SILENT LIGHT, SILENT LOVE

Western Prairie Brides Book Two

D1738392

BOBBY HUTCHINSON

Silent Light, Silent Love
Copyright © 2014 by Bobby Hutchinson

http://bobbyhutchinson.ca/

Publisher's Note: This is a work of fiction. Names, characters, places, and incidents are a product of the author's imagination. Locales and public names are sometimes used for atmospheric purposes. Any resemblance to actual people, living or dead, or to businesses, companies, events, institutions, or locales is completely coincidental.

All brand names and product names used in this book are trademarks, registered trademarks, or trade names of their respective holders. We are not associated with any product or vendor in this book.

This is the second book in the Western Prairie Brides series. The first is LANTERN IN THE WINDOW, also set in the late 1800's, about a mail order bride, Annie, and her deaf sister, Betsy, who come to the Canadian prairies to meet a man who'll change the course of both of their lives.

Silent Light, Silent Love is Betsy's story.

Chapter One

Betsy Tompkins reined in her mare and studied the prairie landscape carefully. She was searching for the perfect sunset photograph, a dramatic study in light and dark. This was probably the best she was likely to find.

She slid off of Jingles' back and dropped the reins to the ground, rubbing the sweat from her face with the sleeve of her blue gingham blouse. As usual, her long mass of auburn curls had come loose from her braid and was hot on her neck. She tried to shove her hair up and back under her sunbonnet, but it was a hopeless task. The late afternoon was hot; even though the wind was building, it intensified rather than lessened the heat.

Jingles nuzzled her back, and she smiled and patted her nose. She'd raised the brown mare from a filly, and Betsy knew she'd stay right where she positioned her. She retrieved her camera from the saddlebag, then walked over to the dry creek bed, squinting off into the distance to find the best visual balance between sky and undulating grassland.

It was late August, the hottest August anyone could ever remember on the Canadian prairies, and there wasn't a trace of green anywhere, although her photographer's eye saw beauty in the undulating yellow and brown grass. The air had a scorched smell, and the sky to the south was red tinged.

Her new Pocket Zar camera captured images in black and white, and she wanted the contrast between sky and land to be distinct and dramatic. She wanted to get a shot of Jingles silhouetted against the sky and the land.

The new camera was her most prized possession, a recent birthday gift from Annie and Noah, her sister and brother-in-law, and their children, her five beloved nieces and nephews.

Betsy still couldn't believe her good fortune in having such a new and innovative device. She could take just one photo at a time, having to retire to a dark spot in the Ferguson farmhouse attic to load another glass plate before a second photo was possible, and she didn't want to waste any of the dozen glass plates that had come with the camera. She'd ordered more immediately, they were available for twenty cents, but having them shipped from far away Chicago could take months. Still, the portability and convenience of the Pocket Zar made her old, cumbersome camera outdated. This one was going to increase her budding photography business, she was sure of it.

She walked further along the bank, looking for a slightly higher spot, a more advantageous angle. Behind her, the wind had picked up, but there was nothing cooling about it. It felt even hotter than the last of the sun's scorching rays, burning through the thin cotton of her blouse. The blue denim pants she'd borrowed from her little stepbrother weren't nearly as hot as a skirt and petticoats would have been, though. Why should men's clothing be so simple, and women's so complicated?

She ignored the heat and took her time. Jingles stood patiently, outlined against the landscape. When she finally decided on the best possible vista, she slowly placed her finger over the lens opening, pulled and held the shutter release lever to one side, removed her finger, and aimed the camera. Then she let go of the lever and her held breath at the same time.

It was only when she drew in a deep lungful of air that she smelled the smoke. Whirling around, she saw a yellowish haze far to the south, low, burning, creeping like a snake over bluffs and little hillocks.

Prairie fire! She let out a startled cry and raced back toward Jingles, who was now tossing her head and turning in restless circles. The horse must have smelled the prairie fire long before Betsy did. She'd been skittish on the ride to the coulee, but Betsy had believed Jingles was objecting to the heat and the far off sheet lightning.

She stowed the camera quickly in her saddlebag, trying to calm Jingles enough to get her booted foot into the stirrup. When she finally managed to swing into the saddle, the horse took off before she could find the other stirrup. She fought with the reins, trying to force Jingles in the direction from which they'd come. That was parallel to where the fire was, though, and the mare fought, dancing and rearing.

Her years of riding stood her in good stead. At last Betsy had the mare racing in the direction of the farm, but she could see the cloud of the advancing fire growing brighter, and the smell of the blue-gray smoke burned in her nostrils. It was travelling faster than she thought possible, and terror filled her.

It was still some distance away, but it looked as if the prairie fire was heading at an oblique angle toward the Ferguson farm-and the wind was increasing.

Noah had gone early into Medicine Hat that morning for supplies. He wouldn't be back until after dark, which would leave Annie and the five children to battle the flames alone if need-be. Their nearest neighbors, the Hopkinses, lived twelve miles to the west. Judging by the ungodly speed at which the fire was approaching, it was unlikely they'd arrive in time to help. Betsy had to get home as fast as she could.

Jingles was still fighting her, pulling at the bit and

trying to turn away from the smoke, and the closer the flames came the more she fought. Neither of them noticed the gopher hole. Jingles' right foreleg went deep into the dirt. She staggered and then fell hard, tumbling to the ground and rolling.

Betsy had a split second to tear her boots from the stirrups before she went flying up and over Jingles' head. She landed on the packed prairie earth, knocking the breath out of her lungs, hitting her head hard on a jutting rock. Pain exploded in her skull and the world spun, turned dark, and then faded away.

Sergeant James Alexander Macleod led his small troop of North-West Mounted policemen across the prairie at a fast pace. He and three other Mounties had been dispatched from the Medicine Hat detachment that afternoon to fight the prairie fire sweeping across the plains. The mounted riders had split up, one heading for the Hopkins farm, and James and his two constables riding full out to reach the Ferguson's, where they hoped to use a team and a plow to dig a firebreak and keep the flames from the buildings should the approaching prairie fire not change course. So far, the wind was not in their favor.

"Thank God you've come." Annie Ferguson shoved her fiery red braid back under her bonnet and hurried toward them as they pulled up in front of the farmhouse.

"The fire's heading this way, and I don't know what else to do."

James saw that she'd already prepared a huge stack of gunnysacks to use to beat at the flames, and a red headed girl and two dark haired boys were frantically pumping water from a well and filling buckets and basins, as well as a nearby horse trough.

"Looks as if ye have things in hand, ma'am."

"My husband is in Medicine Hat, there's just the children and me." Annie's voice was steady, but the strained look on her face and the panic in her emerald-green eyes revealed her terror. The hot wind blew her gingham dress close to her body, and James realized she was pregnant.

"We'll need yer team and a plow, ma'am, to dig a firebreak," James said.

Annie shook her head, and her frustration was evident. "Noah took the team into town before daybreak, and my sister Betsy is off somewhere on her mare. I don't have any other horses because neighbors borrowed our other team two days ago for harvesting."

"We'll use our mounts," James assured her. "We'll need tack. Is it in the barn?"

Annie was already off and running, her hands clasped under her belly, supporting it. The three policemen followed her, dismounting when they reached the large, well-constructed barn.

James, as senior officer, took charge, and the constable's horses were rapidly stripped of their saddles and fitted out with harnesses. The men were hitching the horses to the plow when a brown mare came galloping into the yard. Foam dripped from her muzzle, and her eyes rolled in terror. She was saddled, and James moved slowly toward her, grabbed the bridle, speaking quietly to the animal, calming her with words and hands.

Annie cried out at the sight of the horse, and one hand pressed over her mouth. "Betsy, oh my goodness, where's Betsy? She must be hurt, Jingles would never run off on her otherwise. Please, you have to find my sister, you have to."

"Which direction did the horse come from?" James looked out toward the rapidly approaching flames, trying to guess how much time there was left to try and stop it with a firebreak before it devoured the entire farm. His men were already urging the horses and the plow toward the smoke. James was about to load gunnysacks on Ajax in preparation for smothering the flames. They'd do their best to save this homestead, but if this Betsy lass was directly in the fire's path and injured---she'd need rescue, and quickly, if there was to be hope for her survival.

One of the dark haired Ferguson boys came racing over, his blue eyes huge in his dirty face. "Auntie Bets was going over to the coulee, she wanted to take a picture of the sunset from there, she told me. I'm going to look for her," he said, taking off at a run.

"Halt, laddie," James thundered. The boy slowed, then turned toward him. James waited until he was close, then bent down and looked straight into the anxious blue eyes. "What's yer name, son?"

"Samuel, sir." The boy gulped but bravely held James's gaze. "Samuel Ferguson. Sir."

"Samuel, I am Sergeant Macleod, and I need ye to stay here, young man, there's important work I need ye to take charge of. I want ye to organize a bucket brigade wi' yer brother and sisters, put up a ladder, and begin soaking down the roof of the house and the outbuildings so no sparks can catch. Can I rely on ye to carry out those orders?"

Samuel squared his bony shoulders and stuck his chest out. "Yes, sir."

"Very good. I'm riding out now to bring your auntie back home, Samuel. Can ye give me good directions as to where ye think she might be?"

The boy was smart and well spoken. He gave James concise directions, and after a few quick words with his men, James swung up on Ajax and headed off to find the missing woman.

The fire was closer now. Smoke and the stench of burning grassland smarted in his eyes and nostrils, and Ajax tossed his head and whinnied in protest.

"Easy, boy." James patted the horse's neck, knowing

there was a very slim chance of finding the woman. He was likely off on a fool's errand that could easily result in the death of his horse and himself. But he had to try. He squinted into the smoky heat, trying to see if anything moved in the distance. There was nothing, nothing except smoke and heat and a feeling that every ounce of air was being sucked dry of moisture. It was increasingly difficult to breathe as he rode further and still further in the direction the boy had given him.

It was Ajax who alerted him. The horse turned his head to the right and whinnied, and James caught a glimpse of something blue on the ground, several hundred yards away. He urged Ajax into a gallop, and was off the horse's back and on the ground beside the girl in a few moments.

She was lying half on her side, her right arm twisted up beneath her, poor lassie. She had a mass of wild curly hair, not the true red of her sister, more a reddish auburn. Her delicate face was stark white underneath its sun-kissed gold, and her eyes were closed; long, inky eyelashes curled against her cheek. The scattering of freckles on her nose stood out in sharp relief. Her sunbonnet was askew and there was a deep, bloody gash on her forehead. He was surprised that she was wearing trousers—he'd only seen one other woman in men's garb out here on the Canadian prairie, an eccentric stubborn female who'd homesteaded by herself down Fort Whoop Up way.

He remembered now that the saddle on the brown

stallion had been a Mother Hubbard, not a sidesaddle. This was an unconventional young woman, to ride astride in men's garb. It was a relief to see her eyelids flutter and open after a moment.

"Miss Ferguson?" He spoke in an urgent tone. "Miss Ferguson, we have tae get out of here quickly, can ye sit up?"

She didn't respond except to give him gave him a dazed look. He moved her gently to her back so he could gauge the extent of injury to her arm. He did a fast and thorough examination, concluding that the arm wasn't broken, but the wrist could be. It was difficult to tell with wrists, there were so many tiny bones. She moaned in pain as he moved it so it lay across her chest.

"I'm going to bind yer arm, lass, so we can ride." He untied the blue bandana he wore around his neck, and then propped her against him to secure the wrist firmly against her body. She was silent as he quickly tied the makeshift bandage around her body to immobilize and support it. He was concerned that she'd sustained internal injuries, or some injury to her spine, but there was no real way of telling. Regardless, he was going to have to move her, and quickly.

"Sorry, Miss Ferguson, so sorry to hurt ye, lass, but we're going to have tae ride. Can ye stand?"

He took her uninjured hand and slowly tugged her, first to a sitting position and then to her feet. She moaned and staggered, and he put an arm around her waist, supporting her. Her body stiffened as she tried to pull away, but her legs buckled under her.

There was no time to waste. He glanced over his shoulder at the smoke billowing toward them, and then gathered her up into his arms. She was slender and light, and he was grateful for that, but still it was going to be a fine trick, getting them both up on Ajax. The horse was a well-trained gelding, however, and wouldn't balk.

She still hadn't said anything. She looked bewildered and frightened, and he smiled reassuringly, hurrying over to Ajax. With some difficulty he hoisted her onto the horse, grateful for her trousers. It was much easier to position her astride without the bulk of petticoats and dress, and her body was pliant under his hands, devoid of whalebone corset.

"Hold on tight." He'd put her in the saddle, and she grasped at Ajax's mane, still disoriented and shaky. He kept trying to reassure her with words as he put his foot into the stirrup and swung up behind her.

"Miss Ferguson, I'm Sergeant James Macleod, with the North-West Mounted. Yer horse arrived back at the Ferguson farm without ye. I'm afraid we have to get back there ourselves, and quickly, because the prairie fire is heading this way. Just rest back against me, if ye can."

He put a supporting arm around her, and she winced and cried out as he touched her injured arm. "Sorry, lass.

I'm afraid ye might have broken yer wrist, I've tried to stabilize it, but it's going to hurt on the ride. Can ye tell me if anything else is paining?"

She still didn't respond, and he secured her as well as he could with her back tight against his chest before he signaled Ajax to move. He hadn't been this close to a woman in some time, and he was grateful for the barrier their combined trousers provided between their lower bodies. He was healthy, and he hadn't been near a woman in far too long. Amazing how a man's cock responded instinctively to a female, even in the midst of an emergency. Perhaps not just any female, but this one was young and slender.

Macleod, get yer evil wee mind to the job at hand, man. Think of the fire out there instead of the one in yer breeches.

The huge horse adjusted easily to their weight, and was soon trotting. As the smoke increased, he broke into a canter. The air was scorching hot, and James coughed and squinted into the distance, trying to gauge the progress of the fire. The wind had shifted slightly, but he couldn't tell exactly where the flames were headed because of the smoke.

After that first cry of pain, the woman made no sound, and James concentrated on holding her as close to his body as he could so as to minimize the jolting, should she have internal injuries. Beyond that there was little he could do to make the journey easier.

She was obviously used to riding, and he was relieved when she adjusted automatically to the horse's gait. A thick chunk of her long curly hair blew back into his face, and it smelled like lemons. He brushed it away from his eyes, wishing he could bury his nose in it. Her slender body felt fragile against him, and the absence of the usual whalebone corset made the contact of their bodies that more intimate.

It was ten minutes before the Ferguson farm came into view, and another five before James pulled Ajax to a halt in the yard. Constable Pringle, who'd been dousing gunnysacks with water, came running over, followed closely by Annie Ferguson.

James handed Betsy down to the Constable as gently as he could. "Mind her wrist, I think it might be broken. Better carry her, she's still pretty dazed, she had a right knock on the head."

James dismounted and the boy he'd spoken to earlier, Samuel, took the reins of his horse and headed for the barn. "I'll feed and water him, sir."

"Good lad," James called after him.

"Bring her in here." Annie hurried ahead of the Constable, into the farmhouse. James followed close behind as Annie led the way into a ground-floor bedroom, and Pringle carefully laid Betsy down on the narrow bed.

James turned to Pringle. "Constable, what's happening with yon firebreak?"

"Baynes got back a few minutes ago, he said the wind shifted, so the Hopkins' place wasn't in danger. He and Kormack are plowing the break, but it looks like the buildings here are safe, too. It's veering to the southwest. If that keeps up, it'll burn itself out when it reaches the river."

"Keep up dousin' the buildings just to be safe, Constable. I'll be out shortly."

Pringle hurried away, and James turned again to Mrs. Ferguson, who was tugging off Betsy's boots.

"She has that nasty gash on her head and her wrist must be hurting her. Could ye ask her please where else she has pain, Mrs. Ferguson? She's nae spoken to me at all, I think she may have a concussion, or perhaps she's frightened of me?"

"Call me Annie, please, sir. Betsy's deaf, she mostly talks on her fingers." Annie smoothed back the long, tangled auburn tresses with a loving, gentle hand.

James felt surprise and shock, followed immediately by intense interest as Annie made rapid hand signals to her sister.

Betsy made emphatic gestures in response, limited to using only one hand. She also made sounds, but they didn't approximate speech.

It had been years since James had used sign. He watched closely, picking up several of the words—horse, fell, leg, broken?

Annie smiled and shook her head. "She's most

worried about her horse, sir. I'm telling her Jingles is fine. Betsy thought certain she'd broken her foreleg in a gopher hole."

James's fingers felt stiff and clumsy as he did his best to respond. "I'll have a look at Jingles when I go out," he slowly signed to Betsy, using a combination of the deaf alphabet he'd learned at university and some of the common signs he remembered for certain words. There were differences in Betsy's signs, but the finger spelling was the same. "Will ye please allow me to look at your wrist and that bump on your head, miss? Do ye have pain elsewhere?"

Betsy's shock was evident on her expressive face. Her mouth fell open and her lovely blue eyes widened. Her hand spelled out, "You sign?"

James nodded. "I learned from a professor's wife at Edinburgh University." His fingers were co-operating a little better with each attempt. "She was deaf, and she taught me to sign and finger spell"

Annie was as amazed as Betsy. "You use some of the same signs that Betsy's friend Florence taught her. Before Betsy met Florence, we used our own made up signs, but Florence had gone to a school for the deaf, and she taught Betsy the proper finger spelling and signs."

"Please, can you tell if wrist is broken? It hurts," Betsy told him. "Ribs are sore, not broken, I don't think. One time I fell from hayloft, broke my ribs." She mimed extreme pain. "This time only sore, not bad pain when I breathe like before," she spelled.

"No pain in yer back? Do ye have acute pain anywhere else?" James moved closer to the bed, gently untying the sling he'd fashioned. "Miss Ferguson, I'll try not to hurt ye," he said and signed.

Betsy shook her head. "Not Ferguson. Name Tompkins. Betsy, please. Nothing else broken for sure. Just sore."

"Betsy, my name is James," he said, examining her wrist as gently as he could, allowing Annie to interpret. "James Macleod."

Betsy's uninjured fingers flew. "Your name James Mac----?" She wrinkled her freckled nose and shrugged.

"Macleod," he spelled slowly. "Good old Scots name, same as me father. Grandfather too, come to that." He probed the bones in her wrist, and when he was done he signed again. "I cannae be absolutely certain, but I don't think it's broken. Just badly sprained. Ye're very lucky, Miss Betsy." He smiled at her.

She nodded, signing rapidly back to him with her one good hand. "Lucky you found me," she said. "Thank you."

"The North-West Mounted take a vow to find all lost lassies," he teased. "Now, if ye have something I could use for bandaging," James said to Annie, "I'll bind this wrist tight so it does'nae hurt as much, and perhaps ye could also bring a basin with soap and water so I can have a look at that gash on her head?"

"I'll get it." Annie hurried off.

The moment she was gone, Betsy swung her legs off the bed.

"Need to help with fire," Betsy insisted when James put a restraining hand on her shoulder. "Annie should not run around." She made the graphic sign for pregnancy, hands rounding over her abdomen.

"Me men will have it in hand." James gently pushed her back down on the bed. "Ye need to be still, ye may have a concussion from that blow on the head. The wind shifted, the fire is heading toward the river, where it'll hopefully burn itself out. we need to wash off that cut on yer forehead so I can see how deep it is." The signs were coming back to him now. He didn't have to stop and think before each new word, but he was abominably slow.

Betsy scowled at him, but then she nodded, subsiding reluctantly back on the pillows.

James suspected she probably had a severe headache, and she must also be hurting in various places from the fall from the horse. He smiled down at her. She had the most startling eyes, huge and expressive in her delicate face, emphasized by those long dark lashes. Blood and dirt were streaked across her tanned cheek and down her neck, and there were bits of straw and dead leaves in her thick curling hair.

"Ye have half the prairie in yer hair," he murmured.

He reached out and removed a piece of straw.

Betsy's blue eyes grew even wider and she flinched and narrowed her eyes at him, giving him a suspicious look just as Annie came bustling back in with a basin, a cloth and a bar of homemade soap.

James regretted his impulse, sorry to have alarmed her, also suddenly realizing how dirty his hands were. "I'll go wash while ye clean up that cut, Annie," he said. "I'll be back directly."

In the kitchen, he dipped water into the washbasin on the stand in the corner, turning back his shirtsleeves to thoroughly soap and rinse his hands. He rubbed soap and water over his face as well after he caught a glimpse of himself in the mirror hanging above the washstand. He'd removed his felt western hat and buckskin jacket, and there was a band of white skin above the tan where the hat brim sat. His face was still streaked with grime, and he scoured it again.

"It's a wonder ye did'nae frighten her half to death," he muttered, giving his face yet another sloshing to get rid of the stubborn dirt, and wondering why it mattered so much that Betsy approve of him. "No wonder she's skittish, ye look like a highway man, Macleod."

Back in the bedroom, he wrapped the injured wrist and then examined the gash on Betsy's forehead. Clean now, it was deep and angry looking. Under better circumstances, it should have been stitched closed, but that was out of the question here.

James said, "Do ye have any honey, Annie?"

When Annie brought the pot of honey, James slathered a generous amount in and around the wound and wrapped a narrow length of bandage over it, trying his best to not tangle the cloth too badly in Betsy's hair. It felt springy and silky to his touch, and again reminded him of how long it had been since he'd touched a woman's hair.

"Should be healed in a day or so, there may be a scar but not much of a one. A doctor friend of mine taught me the healing benefits of honey," he assured Annie and Betsy, whose fingers quickly signed, "What you did study at university?"

"Mathematics, the sciences, philosophy," he replied, immediately uncomfortable. "But it was long ago, and a world away."

Six years, two months, and twenty-two days, exactly.

Betsy's fingers flew. "You train as doctor?"

Annie shook her head at her sister and put her finger to her lips. "Sorry, Sergeant, Betsy's questions aren't always polite. She's always been really curious, and questions everything. Without hearing, it's how she learns."

"Of course." James struggled with how to answer without revealing things better kept private. "I craved a bit of adventure, so I signed on with the Mounted," he finally replied, avoiding the question as best he could. "They were promising able bodied men a life more exciting than university."

Betsy was paying close attention. "But being doctor is special," she said. "Why you not want to be doctor? You know how fix my arm, my head."

The lass was too sharp for her own good—or his. "The Mounted expects its members to know a wee bit about many things," James prevaricated. "Jack of all trades," he said.

Betsy started to sign again, but Annie put a hand on her sister's arm and shook her head. "It's not polite to pry, Betsy," she reproved in a soft tone. She didn't always sign when Betsy was watching her, James noted. So, Betsy was adept at lip reading.

Betsy made an apologetic face and rubbed her fist on her chest in the sign for sorry.

"No need for apologies," he said, and he could tell Betsy understood.

He turned to Annie. "Would it be possible for me men and me tae stay wi' you for a day or two? Ye would of course be reimbursed. We'll need to make certain the fire is indeed out before we head back to Medicine Hat."

Annie nodded, her pretty face alight with a welcoming smile. "It would be my pleasure, Sergeant, and my husband Noah's as well. He should be back soon, and he'll be so grateful to all of you for what you did for us. for finding Betsy."

"It's our job. I look forward to meeting yer husband,

mistress."

"There's the couch in the sitting room, but I'm afraid some of you'll have to bed down in the barn. There's no spare bedroom with Betsy visiting. But there's a finished room out there."

"The barn will do very well for us, thank ye, ma'am." James turned so Betsy could see his face. "Ye don't live here, then?"

She shook her head and signed a response. "Live in Medicine Hat."

"Betsy and her friend Rose Hopkins board with Rose's Aunt Harriet," Annie explained. "Betsy works as a seamstress for Miss Evangaline, but she does photography as well. Rose is employed at Gunderson's bakery."

"Yer friend Miss Hopkins is a young woman wi' bonny fair hair? I know of her, she's served me, but we haven't been formally introduced. Their cream scones are a rare treat."

Betsy had followed the conversation closely, and she rolled her eyes and nodded enthusiastically. Then she winced and touched her head.

Annie laughed. "Everyone loves those cream scones, but Mrs. Gunderson won't share the receipt. We're counting on Rose finding out how it's done sooner rather than later."

James realized he'd spent longer than he'd planned with the women. "If ye'll excuse me, I must go and see how me men are faring."

"Supper will be ready in another hour. Nothing fancy, I'm afraid. That fire got me sidetracked," Annie said.

"We shall be most grateful for any food at all," James declared. "Ye must be exhausted, so please, anything at all will do for us." He gave Betsy a small bow and a wink. "I strongly suggest ye stay in that bed for the rest of the day, lass," he told her in a stern tone. "Or I'll need to be havin' ye appear before the magistrate for disobeying orders."

She watched him closely, and he knew she'd understood when she blew a raspberry and shook her head.

"Bossy man," Betsy told Annie. Then she sat up too fast and groaned when her head throbbed. She swung her legs to the floor and then, dizzy and nauseous, grabbed Annie's arm to steady herself. "Ooooh, dizzy."

"You get yourself back in that bed this minute, missy, you saw what the Mountie said," Annie scolded. "And let's get these filthy trousers off of you." She undid the buttons and belt and then scooted the garment off Betsy's legs, drawing up a light blanket to cover her sister's white drawers.

"Bring me skirt, please, I want to help with supper, too many people just for you." Betsy knew what it took to cook for so many people. She'd been helping Annie do it most of her life, and with Annie expecting, she needed to ease the burden for her sister.

"Nonsense. Mary and the twins will help me, and even little Alice is quite good at peeling potatoes these days. if I need more help, I'll call on that handsome policeman of yours." Annie gave her a teasing look.

Betsy shook her head and then grimaced at the pain that shot though her skull. "Not mine. Hearing man. No more hearing men for me ever again." The memory of George Watson's betrayal still hurt, even though it had been more than a year now.

"This one can sign, though," Annie pointed out. "George Watson was a cad, and not smart to boot. As much time as he spent here and with you, he ought to have learned some sign. then to ride off like a thief in the night without so much as a thank you for Noah! He was no gentleman, that was certain. This Mountie is a gentleman. It shows in his speech and manner."

Betsy had never told her sister the details of what Watson had done to end their relationship. "Hearing though," Betsy insisted, using the only excuse that would make sense to Annie.

Annie sighed. "Hearing, deaf, you make too much of that one thing. I don't know what that Watson man did to you, but you mustn't judge all men by one bad egg. You'll end up a spinster, and that's a hard, lonely life." She spoke, signing only the odd word like "spinster" that might be hard for Betsy to catch. "That isn't what you want, Bets.

You need a husband and a family of your own."
Unconsciously, her hand caressed her belly. "And the
chances of ever meeting a deaf man you could love, well,
that's like looking for a needle in a haystack. How many
other deaf people have you ever met? Apart from elderly
people."

It was an old argument between Betsy and her sister.

"Florence. I met Florence." Betsy still wrote to her,
even though it had been months since she had heard back.
What had become of her friend? Florence and her mother
had visited their relatives, the Carlsons, five years ago for
an entire summer. Betsy had been overjoyed to meet
someone young and deaf and female, like herself.

Florence had taught her the proper way of signing.
When the visit was over and she returned to Toronto,
Florence had written often, and then as the years passed,
the letters grew fewer and fewer. In the last one, she'd had
been about to marry a hearing man, a butcher in Toronto.
That was the last Betsy had ever heard from her. She'd
written and told her friend about moving to Medicine Hat,
working as a seamstress, hoping to have her own
photography studio. She'd given Florence her address, care
of Mrs. Coleman's boarding house, but she'd never heard
another thing.

Annie moved to the window. "Jake's barking, I think
Noah's back. He'll be that worried, seeing the fire and all.
I'd better get going with supper, he'll be hungry too. Now,

for once in your life do as you're told and keep your head down on that pillow for the rest of the evening. Stay tomorrow and Monday so you're feeling better before you head back to the Hat."

Betsy shook her head and then grimaced when the movement sent a bolt of pain through her skull. "Have to go back Monday morning, have appointment for family photo," Betsy signed. She was beginning to become known for her portraits. If she was ever to save enough money for her own photography studio, she needed every single customer.

"All the more reason to stay put and recover now, while you can, then."

"You feel alright? Baby is fine?" Betsy's face showed her concern. "You must not work too hard. Try and rest more."

"Don't fret over me, I'm perfectly well, and the baby's fluttering about like a little butterfly, nothing to worry about."

Betsy felt relieved. Annie had miscarried two years ago. She'd been in her third month, and Betsy had been terrified by the quantities of blood and the pain. Noah had been frantic. Annie was almost seven months along now, so maybe the danger was past. Betsy has asked Rose's mother, Gladys, and she'd said that once the third month was past, usually the danger of losing the child was lessened.

"You and Noah, always fretting like a pair of old hens over me." Annie's smile was gentle. "If I needed to rest, I would. But I'm perfectly healthy this time, so stop your worrying."

Betsy could only pray that it was so.

Annie hurried out, and Betsy had to admit that her head hurt like fury. Trying to get up had left her faint and nauseous. Her wrist ached, her ribs hurt with every indrawn breath, and she was beginning to be aware of bruises in other places as well, notably her backside. How could she have landed on her head and still hurt her backside?

Her thoughts went to Jingles. It was a miracle her beloved mare hadn't broken her leg. She'd have had to be put down, and it would have broken Betsy's heart. if Jingles hadn't raced back to the farm for help, she would likely have died in the fire. Love for her horse warmed her heart.

Reluctantly, she admitted that at least part of her gratitude was owed to James Macleod, as well as her horse. She remembered the moment when she'd come to properly and looked up at the policeman. She'd felt incredible relief to have him helping her, and also a sense of strength and safety in his arms, which was strange. Since Watson, she distrusted any man not in her immediate family, yet James's touch, his arms around her, hadn't frightened her. It wasn't fear she'd felt, she admitted now. It was something quite different, something she didn't want to feel for any hearing man.

Her photographer's eye had captured a mental image of his features, and she went over them in her mind's eye one by one. Sculpted high cheekbones, face bronzed by the sun. Lines around his eyes from squinting at the prairie. He had sad eyes, dark brown, unreadable eyes, did James Macleod. They were incredibly intense, as if he could see right through to her thoughts, as if he was looking into her. Straight dark eyebrows, square jaw, neat ears flat to his head, tanned neck. Long arms and legs, wide shoulders. Very strong; he'd lifted her on to the horse as if she weighed no more than four-year-old Nellie.

And he knew how to sign. She still could hardly believe he knew sign language. He was also easy to lip read because he was clean-shaven. So many men wore beards and moustaches, which made it difficult to read their lips.

He was a very tall, good-looking man, she acknowledged to herself. His hair was midnight black, thick and inclined to curl. His wide mouth was quick to smile. His large, rough hands had been gentle on her wrist and on her head. She sensed he was a kind man. She pondered briefly over why he didn't want to tell her more about his education. He'd been uncomfortable when she brought it up. There was a confidence in the way he'd bound up her wrist and treated her head that made her think he was a doctor. Being a doctor brought huge respect and prestige, especially here in the Canadian west. But, then, so did being a member of the North-West Mounted. But why didn't he want to talk about himself?

Curiosity killed the cat, Annie always told her, but how else did people learn?

She'd like to photograph him. His features were bold, shoulders broad, waist and hips narrow. He was wearing a buckskin jacket and grey homespun shirt instead of the scarlet dress she'd noticed policemen wearing in Medicine Hat. His narrow trousers, however, had the distinctive policeman's stripe and were tucked into high, dusty boots.

A handsome man. A man women would follow with their eyes and flirt with. He's hearing, she reminded herself. So don't dream about him, Bets. Remember, never trust hearing men, police or not. Hearing and deaf live in very different worlds.

With that, exhausted and weary, she fell asleep.

"I can't thank you gentlemen enough for coming to my wife's rescue today," Noah said, raising his water glass in a salute to the Mounties gathered around the supper table. "I should have read the weather better than I did and stayed home."

"No one can predict sheet lightning starting a blaze," Constable Pringle said, and all the Mounties nodded in agreement.

The big supper table was crowded with the four

Mounties and Noah and his family. Annie had fed the older children before the adults, and the youngest, red-haired little Nellie, now sat nodding on Noah's lap, sucking at the two fingers she had plugged in her mouth. In answer to James's question as to how old she was, Nellie had shyly held up four of those fingers.

The likeness between the girls and their pretty mother was striking, James thought. It was curious how the girls all had their mother's fiery hair, while the boys were dark like Noah. They were an exceptionally handsome family.

The oldest girl, Mary, was serving the food. She was going to be a beauty, with the same fine features and glorious thick flaming hair as her mother. She was ten, she'd informed him. Her sister Alice was six; her twin brothers Samuel and Charlie, eight.

Noah Ferguson had a fine family. He was also a good farmer, a good provider. The children were well-mannered, clean and clever, obviously loved and well cared for. The homestead was carefully tended, the livestock penned in strong enclosures, the house and barn both spacious and well-constructed. Even the outbuildings, chicken coops, and woodshed had been sturdily built.

James thought Noah was considerably older than his wife, but he was also tall, strong, and good looking, his thick dark hair just starting to turn white at the temples. Judging by the way they smiled at one another, the way Annie's hand lingered on her husband's shoulder, it was obvious this was a love match. Noah had insisted Annie sit down beside him and allow Mary to do the fetching back and forth. He'd seen the girl load a tray and take it in to Betsy. He was relieved that she'd taken his advice and stayed in bed, although part of him also wished she was sitting at the table. He wanted to get to know her better.

The room they sat in was very large, a combination kitchen and sitting room in one. There was a cook stove in the kitchen part, and a big heater at the other end of the sitting room. Two horsehair sofas flanked the stove, with embroidered pillows along their back. A rocking chair sat beside the cook stove, and a dresser held precious bits of china. The walls were papered in pink and yellow flowers, and he'd taken time to study the photographs hung here and there.

Annie had confirmed that Betsy had taken them. They were mostly family photos, but instead of the usual formal poses, these depicted a more casual approach, with the children hugging dogs and cats, Noah with his arm around Annie's shoulders and his youngest in his arms, one of Noah chopping wood. They were all carefully framed in strips of polished wood, and Annie said that Betsy had also made the frames, with some help from Noah.

"Please tell Betsy I had a look at Jingles' leg, there's not a thing amiss with it. The mare came off much more fortunately than she did," James said now to Annie, sitting between him and Noah. He passed her the platter of cold ham, and then the fat loaf of sliced fresh bread. There was also a huge bowl of boiled eggs, jars of pickles, coleslaw, fresh-churned butter. A dish of stewed fruit and a platter of oatmeal cookies were the perfect finale.

"This is a grand meal, Annie, we all thank ye for it," he added. "We'd be eating hard tack and bully beef were it not for you."

The other policemen all agreed, and lifted their water glasses in a toast to their hostess.

Her cheeks turned pink with pleasure, but she waved a dismissive hand at the loaded table. "It's not but a pickup meal, what with the fire and Betsy being lost and all."

"Is she really not badly injured?" Noah asked with a worried frown. "Should we have Doctor Kinsade come?"

"Sergeant Macleod was every bit as good as a doctor," Annie said.

James tensed. He deliberately didn't look at Annie.

"She's sprained her wrist and banged herself up a bit, but I'm certain there's no need to have the doctor come by, Noah," Annie went on. "And she insists she's riding back to Medicine Hat on Monday morning, she says she has photography appointments."

"She's not riding back alone," Noah said firmly. "I'll accompany her. I don't approve of her riding alone across the prairies, I've told her so many times." He turned to James and added, "She's far too independent, is our Betsy." His tone was one of concern and deep affection. "She will ride out by herself, despite that I forbid it."

"Maybe I can help," James suggested. "I'll escort her if that's acceptable. I should check in with Staff Sergeant Osler on Monday and give him a report on the fire."

Not entirely necessary, James knew. Osler wouldn't expect him to ride all the way back to headquarters just to report that he and his men had fought the fire successfully. But it sounded logical enough. Noah was right, it wasn't safe for a woman to ride alone. There were still renegade bands of Indians and not a few outlaws on these western prairies.

But he also knew that wasn't the reason he was offering.

"That would be a great kindness, sir. I thank you," Noah said. "I don't exactly fancy setting off again toward the Hat. One trip a month is more than enough for me."

"It will be my pleasure," James said, startled to realize it would be. The surprising truth was, he very much wanted to get to know Betsy Tomkins. What better way to accomplish that than a long horseback ride across the prairies? He didn't let himself wonder why it was important to get to know Betsy. He just knew it was.

Sunday was a busy day. James and his men tracked offshoots of the fire, using gunnysacks to beat out stubborn flames, and then they split up, delivering the mail entrusted to them to the Ferguson's neighbors, the Hopkinses, and then checking on two new families in the vicinity, making certain they had provisions and were preparing for the coming winter. One of the new settlers reported a small herd of wild stallions in a nearby gulch, and James sent his constables to round them up and take them back to the detachment. Horses were as precious as gold.

It was late evening before he returned to the Ferguson farm, and by the time he ate the stew Annie had put aside for him and helped Noah with the chores, he was more than ready to bed down in the tidy room in the barn where he and his men had spent the previous night. Before he slept, he thought of the following day, when he'd ride with Betsy. He was very much looking forward to it.

On Monday morning, they left the Ferguson farm when only the faintest hint of dawn was showing in the eastern sky.

Annie had made them a substantial breakfast with Betsy's help: oat porridge, bacon, eggs, fresh biscuits hot from the oven. The women talked as they worked, flashing signs rapidly in between chores.

James, who'd helped Noah with the morning chores, also offered the women his assistance. He was told firmly to sit down, drink his coffee, talk to Noah and keep out of their way. He gave Annie a snappy salute and did as he was told.

Before they ate, James saw Betsy have an animated discussion with Noah. Out of politeness James turned his back so he wouldn't see the signs. He was fairly certain she was protesting the fact that he was riding back with her. Noah must have held his ground, because she made no further protest when, after breakfast, James and Noah brought both saddled horses from the barn.

Betsy was still pale, and he'd noticed her wince as she settled into the saddle. She had a fresh white bandage around her forehead, but she'd insisted on taking off the sling on her arm, saying that it felt much better. He'd wrapped her wrist again that morning, far too aware of the tender skin on the inside of her wrist, the way blue veins snaked under her fair skin, the long, tapering fingers with their short nails, the chemical stains from developing fluid on the palms of her hands. Being that close to her, he could also smell her fragrance, a mixture of the lemon scent of her hair, a hint of rose-scented soap and, underneath, an enticing musky odor that was purely Betsy.

He'd been sorry when the bandaging was done. He'd had the most inappropriate and overwhelming urge to take her in his arms.

She rode astride again this morning, but not in trousers. She was wearing a dark green dress with a voluminous skirt that allowed her to arrange the folds modestly, covering her legs. She favored her injured wrist, and although she'd assured him it wasn't hurting much, he didn't believe her. Nevertheless, she used it to loosely hold the reins so her good arm was free to sign.

"How did ye get interested in photography, Betsy?"

The ride ahead was long, and he wanted to take every opportunity for conversation. His signing was coming back, and his fingers were more nimble today. He was also getting better at reading the signs.

"Man came to the door when I was seventeen, asked Noah if he wanted photograph of family," Betsy signed. "I never saw camera before, and when I saw photo, I thought it was magic. Something that didn't need speech to explain, something beautiful that uses only eyes and light."

Bonnie, as are you, lass, James thought. The light was still faint, outlining her profile against the dark sky. He rode close to her so he could see her signs.

"So ye decided then and there ye'd be a photographer?"

She gave him a quirky grin and shook her head. "Never thought possible for deaf girl like me. Then new teacher came to the school, woman teacher, Miss Pettigrew, she let me come to class and borrow books. Some about photography, and teacher say I can be photographer if I want hard enough."

"Before ye were seventeen, ye didn'ae go to school?"

Betsy shook her head. "No time for school before

35

Annie marry Noah. Sister and I work in factory in Toronto after our mother die." She made a face. "Bad place, make me very sick, cough all the time."

The thought of the two girls working in a factory made Noah shudder. He'd heard about the horrendous conditions, the numbers of children who died doing such work. There were many such places in England, and a few even in Scotland.

"And yer father?"

She screwed her face into a grimace and made the sign for drinking. "Not good man, take all our mother's money for spirits. Died when I was five."

"How old were ye when Annie married Noah?"

"Fourteen. Noah try, but schoolteacher back then wouldn't let me go to his school, because I am deaf. But our mother already taught me to read and write when I am little, her father schoolteacher, and Noah's father gave me books, Noah taught me mathematics. Then Miss Pettigrew teach me many things, and I raise baby calf to big steer, sold him and bought camera. Big camera." She made a huge circle with her hand.

Noah laughed. "A steer for a camera, seems a good trade to me."

"Me, too."

Her saucy grin captivated him.

"And now I have small camera, Noah and Annie and children give me for my birthday."

Her enthusiasm and excitement captivated him. Her face reflected every emotion her fingers spelled out.

"Love, love, love little camera. Can carry with me, easy to take photographs." Her passion for photography was evident in every dramatic sign, every animated expression.

She'd looped the reins loosely around the saddle horn now, still using only her uninjured hand to sign. Jingles, well-trained animal that she was, didn't miss a step.

James had to concentrate hard to keep up with the stream of signed words. His own signing, although improving, was still badly out of practice. He understood her easily, but sometimes she giggled when he got what he meant to say totally wrong, and several times he pretended to get it wrong just to hear that deep throated, light-hearted sound.

The horses, left to their own decisions, had agreed on a moderate walking pace, which meant the trip would take much longer than usual, and that suited James fine. This girl—this woman—intrigued and fascinated him. She was so intelligent, so assured in spite of her deafness. She was courageous, determined to make her own way in the world when the accepted course was usually marriage, children, home making.

They'd left at dawn, and for the first two hours it was comfortably cool. They had to make a wide detour around the area where the fire had been, which was also going to add several hours to the journey. The morning grew warmer as they rode.

The prairie was filled with sound: buzzing grasshoppers, singing birds, grass whispering in the breeze. James was aware as never before how much sound there was in his world, and how much silence there must be in hers. But he also noticed as never before the visual beauty, the waving grasses, the birds, an antelope that moved with fluid grace out of their way, the vast blue canopy of sky above them.

"Were ye always deaf, Betsy?" It was a very personal question, and he wondered if she'd take offense.

She shook her head. "Annie says when I was baby, I could hear. Two years old, I have high fever, then deaf."

So no real memory of sound. He was thinking about that when she turned the tables on him.

Chapter Two

"Why you not want to be doctor?" Her head was turned toward him, her expression questioning. Her eyes were so deep and rich in color he was instantly reminded of the cobalt blue stone in the Scots thistle brooch his mother always wore. It had been a gift from James' father on their wedding day, and it gave him a start to be reminded so intensely of his parents and his far away home, here in these circumstances. He usually did his best not to think about Scotland and his family. He'd come away with the intention of leaving that part of him behind forever.

"You like being policeman more?"

"They're very different," he said, realizing even as he signed it that she wouldn't accept that as an answer.

He was right. Her hands were flying before he'd finished the sentence.

"Why not? Doctor really good thing to be. Policeman good, but anyone can be policeman, as long as you are a man. Doctor better, especially when you have much education, university. How many years you go to school, James?" She was frowning at him, her entire face reflecting her curiosity.

It was the first time that morning that she'd used his name, and the intimacy pleased him even as he pondered his response. "I studied for four years at University."

"Long time."

It was a long time—all for nothing. He was silent for a while as the horses plodded on, trying to figure out how to justify the years of schooling, his choice of policing as a career.

"What you will do after you leave North-West Mounted?"

She had an uncanny ability to zero in on everything he was uncertain about. He'd given a lot of thought to what he'd do when his term was up, but he couldn't seem to reach a decision. "I'm not certain what I'll do. The five years I signed on for are up this October."

"Will you sign on five years more?"

"Haven't decided," he said with a shrug.

"Will you go back to Scotland?"

That question he could answer with no qualifications. "Nae. No. That I shall not do, lass."

Her brow puckered. "You are not close to your family, James?"

"I am, aye. I just have no desire to return. It's a long story," he hedged.

She gave him a look. "So?" She waved a hand at the rolling prairie in front of and behind them. "We have much time, yes?"

He nodded and had to laugh at her insatiable curiosity. "Aye, we do, lassie." He'd asked her personal questions, it was only fair to tell her something of his background. Not all—he told no one all of it. He settled on the obvious.

"I grew up in Scotland, in the Highlands. My father is Laird Alexander Maclean," he began. "I have an older brother, Robert, who'll inherit the title of laird and take over the management of the estate, which was why I was free to leave." Lost in his memories, it was a while before he took up the story again.

Betsy waited patiently, her eyes on him. "Only one brother?"

"I had a sister, Marguerite. I was right fond of her," he said, having to clear his throat before he could continue. "She died in childbirth, my wee nephew with her. There were questions as to whether the care she received from the…..the doctor attending was all it might have been. It caused a row in the family, just at a time when we should have drawn together. My father and I had words over it, and I had to leave. That's when I signed on with North-West Mounted."

"Very sorry, James. Hard to have family die. Hurts in your heart."

"Aye, it does that, Betsy." Lost in his memories, he

didn't immediately realize that she'd pulled Jingles to a halt.

"We have lunch over there, yes?" She pointed to low-lying bushes that would provide a modicum of shade. The sun was high overhead. James could hardly believe it was noon; the time had gone so quickly.

She spread a starched snowy cloth on the grass, along with the food Annie had packed.

James tethered the horses where they could graze. The lunch was substantial, ham sandwiches, oatmeal cookies, a stone bottle of cold tea and crisp apples. Betsy was quiet while they ate. When they were done, she reached a hand out and put it on James's arm.

"I am very sorry for what happened with your sister," she signed. "For you and your father, too. Hard to fight. Family very important, hard not to be together."

"Thank you." He placed his hand over hers, surprised at the comfort her simple words afforded him. Would it be different if she knew the whole story? He wrenched his thoughts away from places he couldn't go, just as she turned her hand palm up, and he closed his around it, holding it close for a long few moments, aware of the heightened sensations it roused.

She'd taken her bonnet off before they ate, fanning herself with it. Now her curly hair sprang up around her sun-kissed face like a nimbus. She was innocently lovely, expressive eyes intent on his face, her nose sprinkled with those golden freckles. The long-fingered hand he held was slender and finely formed, as was the rest of her. On impulse, he lifted her hand and pressed his lips to her palm.

She made a startled sound and yanked her hand away. Her cheeks turned fiery red, and there was anger and outright fear in her eyes. She got to her feet and began gathering up their picnic, not looking at him, keeping her distance.

James cursed himself for a gormless idiot. Here they were out in the middle of the prairie, and he was practically a stranger to her. What had he been thinking, taking such liberties?

He went over to her and gently touched her arm, trying to get her attention.

"Betsy?"

She whirled and snatched her arm away, stepping back until she was some distance from him.

"Betsy, I humbly beg yer pardon," he signed rapidly, hoping she'd give him time enough to get through an explanation. "I meant no disrespect, I was just grateful to ye for understanding. I've not told anyone here in Canada about my sister, and it touched me that ye were so gracious. Please don't think I would ever do anything to cause ye concern."

She thought about that for what seemed a long time to James. Then she gave a curt nod and turned away, stowing everything in her saddlebags, giving the cloth an energetic shake and folding it carefully on top of the picnic things.

Her cheeks were deep red, and she wouldn't meet his gaze.

He finally got her attention and said, "My humblest apologies. I do hope ye will trust me again?"

At last she turned back to him, her face troubled. "You are honest with me, I will be with you," she signed. "Man I thought wanted to court me wanted—" she paused, looked away, and then went on, "Wanted something else." Her entire face turned fiery red, but she bravely held his gaze as her fingers spelled out the story. "He try to hurt me, I had hard time fighting with him, got away, but scared me. Makes me afraid now."

The stark and simple words painted a horrifying scenario. As the full import of what she meant sank in, James felt rage building in him. That any man would take advantage of a woman or mistreat her in any way was beyond his understanding, but to think that some—some monster would try to—of course he'd tried to rape her. He wondered how far the assault had gone. He struggled to control his fury, lest he frighten her even more. He took several deep breaths and did his best to control his expression.

"What was his name?" James would make it his business to seek the heathen out and teach him a much-needed lesson. His fists curled in anticipation.

But Betsy shook her head. "Not important, I try not to remember. Would make big trouble, Noah would be very angry, make me stop riding by myself, would try and find man, much, much trouble for everyone." She swung up on Jingles, waiting for him to mount as well. "Noah worries, cares about me. He has big family, doesn't need to worry for me, too."

The fact that she would be more concerned about her brother-in-law than herself touched James's heart. He mounted Ajax, deciding not to pursue the matter. Not now. But he vowed that he would learn who had assaulted her. When he did, he'd beat the bastard to within an inch of his life.

"Noah is best brother-in-law to me," Betsy continued as they rode. "Annie married with Noah, never saw each other, only wrote letters. Annie wouldn't come here from Toronto unless married already."

A mail order bride. Noah knew of several such marriages, some of which were successful. On the whole, he believed most were not.

"Didn't tell Noah I was sister. Said I was daughter, said she was older. Noah wanted older woman. Didn't tell I was deaf. We were very, very scared he would send us back." She smiled and shook her head. "Annie tell him big, big lies in letters, that she can cook, that she know about farming things. But she never saw cow before, she is afraid of chickens." She made the sign for running away, and she giggled.

James had to laugh with her. She had the most engaging giggle, the kind that would stir pleasure in everyone around her. Every moment with her was a delight.

"Never saw farm before, Annie. Never cooked anything but eggs and bacon, potatoes and maybe beans. Annie scared of horses, cows, especially of geese, never gathered eggs or milked. We are city girls, only work all day hard in mill. But Noah tell big lies also. He has father, Zachary, very sick, very cranky, needs much care, Noah never tell Annie. So they are even."

She made the sign for balance, and he nodded, wanting her to go on.

"Very hard at first, Annie's bread, phfft, bad, hard like rock, feed to chickens." She shook her head and screwed up her face. "Zachary throw dishes at Annie, very angry, can't speak, frustrated. Stroke. So I teach him my signs." She smiled sadly. "He teach me many things. Very wise man, Zachary, he and I friends, neither can talk with voice." She made the sign for love, a little way out from her heart, signifying her deep affection for Noah's father. "He teach me to carve, make small animals from soap. He tell me about building house, about his wife, he love her very much, miss her. Then he die. I miss him, bad, bad. Heart aches for him still." She mimicked tear marks down her cheek.

"So Noah and Annie worked things out? Her bread is very fine now." James was enchanted by her flying fingers, her dramatic expressions as she told the story.

Betsy nodded, indicating that Annie had become pregnant. "First Christmas, Mary is born, big storm, no doctor." She rolled her eyes dramatically. "Noah and I help Annie. Noah has book on how babies are born." She pantomimed Noah frantically flipping pages and wiping sweat from his forehead, his hands trembling and hers as well. "I am so scared, Noah too. But Mary is okay, Annie too. Noah and I—" She held a hand out flat and tipped it from side to side as if it was touch and go with them, and again, Jamie laughed. He could well imagine how traumatic that birth must have been. A first delivery, as well. They'd been very lucky.

"All other babies, Noah has doctor come to farm every day when time is near." Her face grew somber. "Two years ago, Annie loses baby, three months. Very bad, we all cry, Annie sick for long time, before baby comes and after. This time, maybe will be better, Annie not sick all the time like she was then."

"When is the babe expected?"

"End of November."

She was nearly seven months along. "If she's feeling well, surely that's a sign all will go well?" He wanted to reassure Betsy. He couldn't keep his eyes off her. She was so vibrant, so alive and animated. Uninhibited, which was so refreshing.

James thought of the other young women he'd met here on the prairies, and also back in Scotland. More of them in Scotland than here in Canada—there was a definite shortage of eligible women on the prairies. But in both countries, there was a strict code of conduct for ladies, and most of them adhered to it. Unfortunately, in his opinion, it made them boring.

Passion wasn't something young women generally demonstrated. It wasn't considered lady-like or polite to even mention pregnancy, much less discuss the actual birth with a man. Betsy's deafness made her refreshingly open, and James found it fascinating.

He was powerfully attracted to her. He mustn't let her suspect, though, if her earlier skittish reaction was any indication. What had happened to her had made her wary of men. If she guessed he had feelings for her, she'd likely never let him near her again, he was fairly certain of that. More than anything, he wanted to gain her trust.

The truth was, he was desperately lonely, tired of the unsettled life of a North-West Mounted policeman, uncertain of what the future held for him. He had no intention of ever going back to Scotland, so he must somehow make a new life for himself here in Canada. As a younger son, there was no responsibility such as his older brother, Robert, had to take over the family estates. He was at a crossroads in his life, and he couldn't figure out which route to take.

He'd never been sorry for the decisions he'd made, joining the North-West Mounted, coming to Canada, but he sorely missed the kinship of the family he was estranged from. The life he led as a mounted policeman was rough-and-tumble. Because of the strict military discipline, barracks were clean but stark, the food nourishing but uninspired, the conversation often course and banal.

The Ferguson homestead had reminded him painfully of what it was like to live in a comfortable, well-ordered house, with the soft and colorful touches only a woman could create. It had reminded him of what was lacking in his life.

Betsy's deafness bothered him not at all. Signing was coming back quickly, now that he had reason to use it, and he knew it wouldn't inhibit their relationship; it was a complex and multi-layered language, with nuances just as subtle as the English language. He felt it could only enhance a relationship, that the few areas where deafness might present difficulties could easily be managed with intelligence and patience.

His mother had always said that no one knew the reasons for what happened in their lives. Thinking back now on his friendship with Calum Fraser and his wife, Fiona, James marveled that learning to sign from Fiona should impact his life so powerfully now.

As they reached the outskirts of Medicine Hat, he determined that he would find every means at his disposal to further his friendship with Betsy. He'd go slow and win her trust. He hoped as well that he could win her heart, because she'd pretty much captured his.

Betsy led the way through town to Liposki's livery stable where she kept Jingles. The owner, a barrel-shaped giant with a gleaming bald pate came hurrying over as Betsy dismounted, taking the reins from her and patting Jingles fondly.

"'Allo, Miss Betsy," he bellowed. "I'll take 'er from 'ere, miss, don't you worry none, we'll take good care o' her fer ye."

Betsy smiled at him and said, "Thank you," using both voice and sign.

James had dismounted as well, and now walked with her, leading Ajax, as she headed down the main street and along a side street to an imposing old brick house set back from a garden which seemed an indiscriminate combination of flowers and vegetables.

"Mr. Liposki thinks I will hear if he hollers loud enough," she told James with a shake of her head. "Many people think same."

"There's a young French-speaking lad at the barracks. He says the same—that by hollering, folks believe he'll ken what they say."

She looked at him, surprised. "I never think hearing people might have same problem."

"Problems aren't limited to the deaf, lass."

They were at the sturdy wooden gate leading in from the street, and she turned to James and signed formally, "Thank you very much for bring me home, James."

Another moment and she'd be gone. He had to manufacture a reason to see her again. "I would like a photograph to send home to my mother," he improvised. "Would ye be kind enough to make one for me, lassie? Sooner rather than later. I could be off on police business at a moment's notice."

It was all he could come up with on the spur of the moment, and he held his breath as she thought it over. "It would be a business agreement, of course," he added. "I'd insist on paying well."

She nodded, as if that was taken for granted. "I have appointment late this afternoon. You could come this evening?"

He breathed a sigh of relief. "What time? And where do ye have yer studio?"

She shook her head. "No studio yet, maybe soon. Mrs. Harriet lets me use upstairs parlor, so come here, eight o'clock?"

"Aye, I shall look forward to it." He considered proffering his hand and decided against it. Instead, he tipped his hat and mounted Ajax.

"Take care of that wrist, Betsy. See you at eight." Now all he had to do was hope Staff didn't have a pressing reason to send him straight back out of town.

Chapter Three

At five before eight that evening, James once again stood at the wooden gate. He'd washed, shaved and changed from his work uniform and was wearing the formal scarlet tunic, blue trousers and white helmet that constituted the Mounted dress uniform.

He walked down the cobbled path and knocked on the door.

A tiny woman, as round as she was high, opened it before he'd even moved his hand away.

"Good evenin', sir, and who might you be?" Her plump face was wreathed in smiles, and her voice was welcoming, with a touch of Scots burr that delighted him.

James snapped off a salute and removed his helmet. "Sergeant James Macleod, mistress. I have an appointment wi' Miss Tompkins for a photography session."

"Well, come in with ye, then. Do I hear a wee hint of the Scots in your voice, Sergeant James Macleod?"

"Aye, that ye do, mistress. Though years away from hame have lightened the burr, more's the pity." James deliberately intensified his accent, and a burble of laughter bubbled from her as he followed her in and down a short hallway to a small living room so crammed with furniture there was barely room to navigate around it.

"It's that pleased I am to meet a bonny man like yerself from the auld country," she said. "Sit yourself down. I'm Harriet Coleman. Now tell me where it is ye're from exactly?"

"Fort Augustus in the Scottish Highlands, Mistress." James removed his helmet, resting it on his knee. "No in the town, some distance outside. My father has a holding some ten miles from the Fort, but me brothers and I attended school at the Abbey."

"Me mother, God rest her soul, was born in Edinburgh, as was I," Harriet said. "We came out with me father to Canada when I was a wee lass, but I remember the auld place well." She motioned at an overstuffed sofa covered in purple velvet. "Sit yerself down and I'll tell Betsy ye're here. Ye must come and take tea with me soon and we'll have a wee natter about hame."

"Aye, it would be my great pleasure, Mistress Coleman." And another way of getting to see Betsy.

She waved a hand at him. "Away wi' ye, it's just Harriet."

"Thank ye, and ye must call me James."

She simpered, blushed and bustled out and a moment later Betsy appeared.

James shot to his feet, and his helmet rolled to the floor.

He bent to pick it up, and then smiled at her.

"Betsy, good evening. Ye look very fine indeed." The compliment was out before he could harness his fingers. She'd changed into a blue dress that mirrored the deep cobalt of her eyes, and her glowing hair was gathered up high in a roll, but curly strands had escaped and were framing her face. Her nose was sunburned. He could hardly tear his gaze away from her.

Her neck was long and slender, the upswept hairstyle becoming. She'd traded the bandage on her forehead for a white sticking plaster that emphasized the gold of her skin. The dress she wore bared a few inches of her throat, and he could see the pulse beating there. The fabric clung softly to her shoulders, outlined the generous swell of her breasts. He could imagine all too easily the fullness of those breasts, the softness of her skin, the long, slender legs under the full skirt.

He realized he was staring.

She flushed slightly and then smiled. "You too, beautiful. Very nice uniform."

Their gazes locked for a long moment, and the room suddenly felt charged, as if an electric storm was imminent. Then Betsy drew a shaky breath, looked away and took a step back.

He needed to lighten the atmosphere. He clamped his

helmet on his head backward crossed his eyes at her and saluted smartly.

"Sergeant Macleod, North-West Mounted, at yer bidding, ma'am."

She giggled, as he'd hoped she would, then beckoned him to follow her up the stairs and along the hallway. She led the way into a long, narrow room with a wide window along its width that looked out on a huge cottonwood tree. She'd set up a backdrop of painted scenery at the far end of the room with an ornate wooden armchair in front. A large camera on a tripod was positioned a few feet away.

"You like to stand or sit, James?"

"Stand, if ye please." He walked over and looked at the backdrop. It was painted on canvas stretched over a wooden frame, a mountainous scene with a stream bubbling through a stand of trees in the foreground. It was realistic and very well done, the colors both subtle and bold.

"Did ye do this, Betsy?"

"Yes, I do six, all different, to suit whoever is having picture taken." She gestured at a stack of other backdrops against the wall. "You can choose another if you want."

James looked through them. There was a flower garden in full bloom, a depiction of a sitting room with a fire in the grate, a lake with a guesthouse on the far shore, a winter scene with snow and sleds, and a ladies boudoir with chaise longue and draped shawls.

Teasing her, he gestured at this last one. "What do ye think of this one?"

She raised an eyebrow. "I like. But what will your mother think?"

"Yer right, the one you chose will do me very well." He moved over to it and suddenly felt self-conscious. "What do ye want of me, lass? How should I stand?"

She came over to him, took his arm and moved him at an angle to the camera. She positioned him in front of the backdrop, took his helmet and tucked it under his right arm. Her touch was businesslike, and she tilted her head and studied him, eyes narrowed.

"Do I look straight at the camera, or off to the side?" He was beginning to feel ridiculous.

"Look toward window, and think of something you like, that pleases you. Hold very still till I say done."

He straightened his back and looked toward the window. He thought of kissing Betsy, and when that fantasy began to progress to more than kissing and be less than comfortable, he forced himself to think of a loch near his home where his brother and he had fished when they were children. It was less exciting, but also less likely to embarrass him. The dress trousers to his uniform were close fitting.

She'd disappeared under a black cloth behind the camera, and he could hear it clicking at regular intervals. It seemed to take an inordinately long time, and his self-consciousness grew.

She ducked back out after an eternity and indicated a different pose for him, with one of his legs propped on a papier-mâché rock she unearthed from a closet. She put his helmet on his head, and he did his best to hold the pose. By now he felt an utter buffoon. One more pose followed. She whipped the backdrop away and had him sit on the armchair in front of a plain board painted a soft creamy shade.

James was sweating by the time they were done, vastly relieved that the photography session was over. He'd exerted less nervous energy subduing fights in a saloon. He used his handkerchief to mop his brow, and when he glanced at Betsy, she was laughing at him.

"So ye think this is funny, do ye? Terrifying a member of the North-West Mounted wi' yer wee black box?" He took a mock menacing step toward her, and she ducked behind the camera and held up her hands, palms out, still laughing.

"I need ice cream to recover," he told her. "Will ye no accompany me to Dunlap's Ice Cream Parlor, Betsy? It's the least ye can do after putting me through this ordeal."

Her smile faded, and she took several moments to respond. At last, she hesitantly moved one fist up and down in the sign for yes, and he expelled the breath he'd been holding.

As soon as she'd agreed, Betsy wished she hadn't.

This tall, incredibly handsome sergeant was dangerous for her. She'd known that ever since he'd picked the stick out of her hair after her fall. His touch on her skin sent bolts of awareness shooting through her. When he'd kissed her palm after their picnic, the touch of his lips on her skin had made heat gather in her private parts. As if the physical attraction wasn't enough, there was the seductive fact that she could talk to him easily and spontaneously. His ability to sign still astounded and amazed her, and even in a few short days, his signing had become much faster, more relaxed and natural as he remembered the language and used it more.

She'd never had that with any man except the males in her immediate family. Communication was a problem with those who didn't sign, and that took in most of the people she'd ever met. It made for a solitary life and, yes, she admitted that she was often very lonely, much more here in Medicine Hat than with her beloved family on the homestead. Having Rose here helped, but she was careful not to monopolize her friend. Rose had hearing friends that she liked to spend time with, and Betsy respected that.

In the city, there were of course older people who'd lost their hearing, but so far she hadn't met a single young person who was deaf like her. Her deafness made people uneasy.

Rose had insisted at first on including Betsy in her own busy social life of dances, card games, picnics, skating parties. But Betsy had seen how most of the other young people avoided sitting near her. A few brave young men had danced with her at socials...she knew she was a good dancer, because she could feel the music's vibration through the soles of her feet and in her chest. But when the music stopped, she sensed the tension in them, the fear that they would have to talk to her, and they didn't know how. They were afraid that they wouldn't understand if she tried to talk to them.

She was good at lip reading, but when she used voice to respond to whatever they were saying, they looked embarrassed and moved away from her.

She'd asked Rose once how her voice sounded, because they had an agreement that they'd always tell one another the absolute truth about everything, even if it was uncomfortable.

Rose had said sometimes Betsy sounded too loud, and sometimes not. So she'd tried to modulate her vocal efforts, but she had no idea how to go about it.

So it was an enormous relief and a great joy to be able to speak freely to James, to have him tease her, laugh with her, understand her without effort.

Which was exactly why it was a mistake to be walking down the street beside him in the evening twilight, heading for the ice cream parlor. Nothing could come of whatever this powerful feeling was between them.

In the end, he belonged to the hearing world. Now, she was a novelty, someone to practice his signing skills with. But she knew the time would come when he would naturally want to be with women like himself, hearing women. She knew that, but just for this one hot summer evening, she couldn't resist walking out with him, pretending they were just like any of the other couples strolling idly along the sidewalks, arm in arm.

Dunlap's was a favorite spot in the heat of the autumn evening, and they were fortunate to find a table free. James escorted Betsy to it and then went to the counter for the strawberry ice cream sodas they'd agreed on. He attracted a fair amount of attention in his formal uniform, and the dark-haired young woman who took his order smiled at him flirtatiously.

"Here you go, Sergeant. Sweets for the sweet," she murmured brazenly, smiling up at him and brushing her hand against his.

He'd become accustomed to the effect uniforms seemed to have on the female sex, and he'd perfected a friendly but aloof response. He smiled at the woman and paid, and then took the brimming sodas and tall glasses over to the table.

In his absence a young and very pretty blonde woman

had taken the seat across from Betsy, and their fingers were flying.

James recognized her from the bakery. He set the sodas down and found a spare chair from an adjoining table, waiting to be introduced before he sat down.

"My very good friend, Rose Hopkins," Betsy signed, adding, "Sergeant James Macleod, he and other policemen fight the fire at home."

Rose was obviously very comfortable with sign, and she signed and spoke to him at the same time, so Betsy was part of the exchange.

"How do you do, Sergeant? A pleasure to meet you, and so many thanks for keeping the prairie fire from burning down Betsy's and my family's farms."

James bowed over the soft hand she offered. "My pleasure, Miss Hopkins. I'm glad we were able to keep the fire away from the homesteads, but it was actually the wind that did most of the work. The fire headed toward the river and burned itself out.   Can I get you a soda or a cone?" He followed Rose's lead, signing as he spoke.

"No, thank you, I'm meeting someone. I'm just a bit early, Sergeant Macleod."

"James, if you please."

"And I'm Rose."

Betsy signed at a furious pace, filling Rose in on the fall she'd taken and the fear they'd all felt at the approaching prairie fire. She held out her injured wrist and described with dramatic gestures how James had come to her rescue, and how the other policemen had dug firebreaks using their horses to pull the plow.

"You hurt your head as well, is it very painful?" Rose asked, reaching a gentle finger out to touch the sticking plaster.

"James put honey on, heal very fast," Betsy replied.

James was struck again with the grace and beauty of sign. It was often so much more expressive than words could be.

"Is Annie feeling well?" Rose was obviously concerned. "I hope all that excitement didn't make her ill."

"She is fine, baby moving all the time. Strong kicks."

Rose laughed. "That's wonderful. Did you feel it kick?"

Betsy smacked one hand against the other, demonstrating how strong the baby was.

Rose seemed as open and comfortable discussing Annie's pregnancy as Betsy was.

Rose turned to James, still signing. "You rode back with Betsy, she told me. I'm glad, I worry about her every minute when she rides all that way alone across the prairie," Rose said to James.

"Worry wart," Betsy accused, with a fond smile.

A tall young man came in the door just then, and when he located Rose, his face lit up. He smiled and waved and came over to their table.

"Hi, Betsy," he said, with a small wave of his hand as Rose got up and looped an arm through his. The glance the two exchanged was electric.

"This is Philip Amundson." Rose, her cheeks flushed now, quickly introduced James to the blond man. James got to his feet and shook hands.

"Do ye care to join us?" James hoped they'd refuse, but manners dictated that he ask.

"Thank you, but we don't want to intrude," Philip said.

"We're going to get in line or we'll never get our sundaes," Rose added quickly. "And yours are going to go flat unless you hurry and devour them."

For a few moments when they were alone, James and Betsy concentrated on the sodas.

"Rose and Philip, courting," Betsy confided, taking another long sip of her drink.

"Aye, I guessed as much. What does Philip work at?"

"He is lawyer, works with his father, also lawyer."

James remembered seeing the sign on Front Street, Amundson and Son, Barristers at Law.

"Not comfortable with me, Philip." She wrinkled her nose and shook her head. "Makes him nervous, me and Rose signing. I think always he worries we are talking about him."

"And are ye?"

She giggled and wrinkled her nose. "Only half the

time."

"Well, if they're courting, he'll simply have to learn to sign, won't he? Or else go through his life worryin' what you and Rose are saying about him."

A huge smile came and went, and then a pensive expression came over her face. "Many people feel same as Philip, nervous when around me. Mostly, I stay home, not ever come here on my own."

Her touching honesty tugged at his heart. He knew that what she was saying was true. Fiona Fraser had explained that very same reaction, that most people withdrew instead of trying to communicate. Fiona had described it as isolating.

"Folks generally feel the same about me, if I'm in uniform like this," James said. "I make them nervous, they're afraid I'll arrest them for something they've done."

"Not all people," Betsy shot back. "Women—" she rolled her eyes and made the sign for love you, curled hands held close to her breasts, and then blushed furiously.

So she'd been watching closely when he bought their refreshments. Nothing much got by her. "Aye, it's a terrible problem," he told her seriously. "Lasses of all ages throw themselves into me arms, professing eternal love. Very difficult for me."

For a moment, she seemed taken aback. Then she realized he was once again teasing.

"Big problem," she agreed with a straight face. "Must

be hard to choose between them."

"No so hard as all that." He let his eyes wander over her lovely features. "Lads generally prefer to be the ones doing the choosing."

She was still blushing, and she avoided his gaze. "Noah told me same. I ask him about men, how they feel, how they choose women. He say mostly women do choosing, but men think it's them."

James laughed. "Yer brother-in-law is a canny man. He's absolutely right about that."

"How old are you, James?"

"Thirty-four."

"Twenty-four."

So he was ten years older than her. Was it too much of a gap? . And you, Betsy?" He'd figured out she must be in her early twenties, and her reply confirmed it

"Do I seem quite ancient to ye then, Betsy?" He tensed, waiting for her answer.

She tipped her head to the side and pretended to study him closely. "No white hair yet, got some wrinkles though. How come you never marry, James?"

Once again, her sense of humor and forthright honesty took him by surprise, and he considered the question carefully before he replied.

"My mother and father have been married for thirty-nine years, and they still love one another deeply. Finding someone ye could be happy with like that for the rest of yer natural life is no easy chore, but it's what I want. It does make finding a suitable lass difficult."

He looked into her wide blue eyes. "I would like nothing more than to find someone wi' whom to share my life. I would like to have a home and a few bairns. Being a policeman is a lonely life, and I have no aspirations to move up in the ranks. I've enjoyed my time as a policeman, but now I would much rather buy land and homestead."

He was making a declaration to her, and he wondered if she'd recognize and acknowledge it. He'd toyed with the idea of being a farmer, but not until this moment taken it seriously.

She shook her head at him. "Farming hard work. That is what you want?"

"My father and his father before him were farmers," he assured her. "Their livelihood to this day depends on sheep and cattle, as does the livelihood of the others on our land. I'm familiar with the hard work involved. I like the Canadian prairies fine, I would like to homestead here." The idea grew on him even as he said the words.

He was watching her reaction closely. "What about you, Betsy? Is marriage and a family of yer own what ye want?"

She thought a moment. Emotions flickered across her expressive features, regret and sadness. "Always I thought when I grow up I would marry and have babies, I love babies. Now, I see is not for me. No young deaf men here.

So I will make my own life, be photographer, have studio, make money, maybe travel to New York someday and see galleries. Spinster, yes?"

Her answer shocked him. "Ye've decided ye will only marry a deaf man, Betsy? Why is that?"

Her face set in stubborn lines. "Only deaf understand deaf. Too hard to be together, deaf and hearing." She bumped her fists together, indicating conflict. "Always problems, deaf and hearing. Not fully understand each other. But no young deaf men in Medicine Hat. So I will be spinster."

James chose his words carefully, taking care with his signing. This could be the end of their relationship, and he very much didn't want that. "Calum Fraser," he began, "the university professor whose wife, Fiona, was deaf, the lady who taught me sign. They had a very happy marriage. Calum was fluent in sign, so there was no barrier between them."

"He can sign and hear. But she can only sign, so yes, there is barrier." Her chin was set, her lovely eyes shuttered.

He shook his head. "Not that I ever witnessed, Betsy. They loved one another. They were one of the happiest couples I ever met."

She shrugged and looked away from him. "Maybe can happen. But not for me." She was very definite. She finished the last sip of her drink. "I think time to go home now," she said.

"Aye, of course." His heart was heavy as he got to his feet and held her chair, helping her up.

Rose and Philip were sitting a few tables away, and they waved. "See you at home," Rose signed to Betsy.

The walk back to Mrs. Coleman's house was mostly without conversation. James frantically sought for some way to make her see what he believed was possible, but couldn't find the words.

When they reached the gate, James opened it and walked Betsy to the door.

"Thank you for my ice cream, and for good conversation," she said formally, holding out her hand.

"T'was my pleasure, lass." James took her hand in his. "I enjoyed it very much." He took a chance and added, "I do hope ye'll allow me to escort ye again, Betsy?"

She looked at him and raised her eyebrows, but she didn't pull her hand away. "Why?"

To James, the simple question seemed to mark a turning point in their relationship. He could make some polite response, or he could simply say what had been on his mind for the past hour.

"Because, lass, I want us to get to get to know one another." And without consciously forming the idea, he heard himself say, "Because I plan to court ye." Saying it made it real, and he realized it had been in the back of his mind ever since he'd first met her. "Because I know ye're wrong about deaf and hearing not being a good combination. I'll prove that ye're wrong."

Chapter Four

Betsy snatched her hand away and shook her head. Her cheeks were bright pink. "Friends, yes. Courting no. I told you, I am not marry hearing."

"And what if I were deaf, Betsy? Would that be different? Would that one thing make a difference, or is it something else about me, besides me not being deaf, that doesn't appeal to ye?"

Confusion made her hesitate. "No," she signed, and then shook her head and ducked her chin. "Yes, if you were deaf, would be different. Only that you are hearing, nothing else." She refused to look at him, and hot color stained her neck and cheeks.

"Betsy." He tipped her chin up gently with one forefinger. He was smiling. "Betsy, could we no just pretend I'm deaf?"

Between one moment and the next, she was furious. Hot color stained her cheeks and her body stiffened. She narrowed her eyes at him and her fingers moved like daggers, slicing the air with passion. "You think is joke, being deaf, you think something you can pretend? Hearing can never imagine what deaf is like, just like hard for deaf to think what hearing might be. Not bad, not good. Just different."

"Aye, but there are differences between all couples," he tried to explain, taken aback at her vehemence.

"Deaf is big difference," she insisted. "Too big."

Damnation. He'd made a grievous mistake. How to rectify it?

"Will ye at least think about it, Betsy? I'll call on ye in a couple of days, we can talk about it again. Besides, there's my photograph, no?"

She thought that over and gave a tiny nod.

It was a small concession, but it left a door ajar. More than he deserved, daft bugger that he was. "Good evening, then, Betsy. I very much enjoyed our time together. I'll see ye again in two or three days."

With another barely perceptible nod, she opened the door and went inside, closing it softly behind her.

Betsy was shaking. She stood in the hallway for several moments, trying to get control of herself. James Macleod affected her in a way no other man had ever done, and it was unsettling.

Noah had a magnet that he used to find nails he'd dropped in the farmyard. Around James Macleod, she felt like one of those nails, drawn inexorably toward the magnet that was James, despite her resistance.

"You're home, dearie. Did ye have a good evening?"

"Hello, Aunt Harriet. It was fine, thank you." She managed a smile, and she hoped Harriet didn't see how flustered she was.

The landlady didn't sign, but she always made sure Betsy could see her face when she spoke, and she spoke naturally and clearly, so she was easy to lip-read. She also understood when Betsy answered with voice. Betsy was very fond of her, and she knew Aunt Harriet felt the same.

"If ye'd like a wee bite before bed, I've fresh scones and tea in the kitchen."

Any other time, Betsy would have loved scones and tea. Tonight, her stomach felt upset, and she shook her head. "Thank you, but long day. Need sleep."

"Away up wi' ye, then, lassie. Rest well."

Betsy climbed the stairs and went into her room. She filled the basin with water and washed top to toe before she donned her nightgown. Her body was bruised and her hips and bottom and injured wrist ached. Her head was hurting again as well.

She climbed in between the fresh linen sheets, sighed deeply as she relaxed, and mentally went over the conversation with James.

He wanted to court her. His declaration, made so soon after meeting her, was shocking. Exciting, too, though it galled her to admit it.

A mental image of him filled her thoughts, and when she envisioned his broad-shouldered, slim-hipped body, tall and strong, an involuntary shiver went through her. His face was clear as a photograph in her mind. His skin was brown from the sun, and always his piercing dark eyes had that trace of sadness. There were lines around his eyes and mouth. She wondered what had put them there. He'd trusted her enough to tell her a little about his life, and that had helped her trust him in turn—or at least, trust him a little back, she amended. She still didn't really know him.

She imagined what it might be like if he kissed her. Outside of her family, only two men had kissed her, one at a church social when she was heading for the necessary, grabbing her from behind and pressing sloppy wet lips on hers even as she struggled. He smelled of spirits, and she'd smacked his face hard, realizing that he was the husband of a neighbor woman she knew well. That he had taken such liberties had shocked and sickened her, but she wasn't frightened. The fool could barely stand up, he was so potted.

The other was George Watson. Even thinking his name made her belly feel a little sick. He'd frightened her badly, and remembering even now brought a trace of that fear back.

Noah had hired Watson the previous fall, to help with the haying. Watson, too, had been good looking, sturdy and very strong. He took his meals with the family and bedded down in the room in the barn that Noah had fixed up for the times he had to hire help, or people stayed over.

George was unfailingly courteous and friendly, and Noah and Annie had encouraged her to accept when he invited Betsy to go to a dance with him.

She'd heard Rose talk about the dances held at the school, and she'd wanted to go. George hadn't made much effort to learn even basic sign, but Betsy hoped maybe he would. She was excited, thrilled to have a good-looking man as her escort. He'd borrowed the buggy from Noah, and Annie helped her make a new dress out of green cotton patterned with tiny daisies.

The evening was magical at first. Noah told her she looked pretty, and she knew it was true. When they arrived at the hall, Rose was there, and Betsy felt comfortable, because the crowd included many of their neighbors, kind people she'd known most of her life. Her dance card was filled almost immediately, and she loved to dance, feeling the beat of the music through the soles of her thin slippers. Rose had taught her the steps long before, and for once she felt like every other young woman there, spinning and laughing, giving herself over to the beat of the music.

George had claimed many of her dances, and when the music was slow, he pulled her close. She enjoyed the feeling of his strong body pressed to hers, although she pulled back when his embrace became too intimate. She could smell that he'd been drinking, but so had most of the young men. She'd noticed him with a group of them, talking and laughing. Once or twice they'd looked her way, and she wondered what they were saying, but she was having too much fun to be suspicious.

They'd ridden home under the stars, and when they reached the farm he took her gently in his arms and kissed her. She'd enjoyed his kisses, they'd awakened a passionate hidden part of her, and she dreamed of him when at last she went up to her room, dreams that made her blush when she sat across from him at breakfast the next morning.

After that, he'd arranged several outings: a church picnic, horseback rides, walks in the evening to the coulee and back. His signing was still very minimal, but he'd held her hand, and kissed her often. He awakened a hunger in her, both physical and emotional, and she began to imagine a life with him, children, a home of her own.

The day came when the haying was done. George would be leaving the next morning. He asked her to ride out with him that evening when the work was finished, and she'd known that he would ask her to marry him.

They'd ridden to their favorite spot, a place near the river where the willows overhung the banks. He'd spread a blanket, and he patted the spot next to him. She sat beside him. He kissed her, and she responded. His hands went to her breasts, fondling her nipples, and she allowed it because of the pleasure it gave her. His hands went to her skirt, and she shook her head no. He tried again, more forcefully this time, and she restrained him again, treating it as a teasing game.

But then his eyes narrowed, his face turned an ugly shade of red, and he swore at her. He grabbed her shoulders and twisted his body, flipping her roughly on to her back, yanking her skirt up almost over her head.

Shocked, taken totally by surprise, she'd struggled against him, and he'd slapped her viciously across the face, once and then back again, holding her down, tearing at her pantaloons. Her eyes filled with tears at the force of the blows, and her cheeks burned.

It had happened so quickly Betsy could hardly believe it was real. But as his rough hands tore at her underclothing and then fumbled with his own trousers, she absolutely knew that unless she did something and quickly, he was going to rape her.

And like a miracle she remembered then what Rose's mother, Glady's Hopkins, had told the girls one rainy afternoon. Rose, giggling in embarrassment, had signed her mother's words as Glady's spoke them.

"If ever any man gets fresh with you, you just use your knee on his bollocks, hard as ever you can. It'll stop him right enough, he won't be able to walk for a bit and he'll be sick as a dog," she'd said, all the while rolling out pie dough with energetic sweeps of the rolling pin. "Every young girl needs to know that," she'd added. "Better safe than sorry, men being what they are."

Remembering now, and going against every instinct, Betsy stopped struggling. She let her limbs go limp.

"That's right, you stupid deaf bitch, you know you want it," she'd read on his lips, spittle flying down on her face. "I told the fellows that you've been asking for it, you deaf and dumb idjit."

He reached down and undid his fly, straddling her, and in that instant Betsy brought both knees up as hard and fast as she could. She connected, and his face contorted. She rolled out from under him, sobbing as she ran for Jingles, her legs barely able to carry her.

She glanced back, terrified that he was after her, but George was rolling around on the ground, retching. Betsy climbed on her horse, and at the last minute, reached out and took the reins to George's horse, leading him behind her and Jingles. It was a good five miles back to the house. Let him walk—when and if he was able.

Her first instinctive reaction was to ride for home as fast as she could and tell Annie and Noah what had happened. But as she rode sobbing and trembling through the dusky evening, she thought about the words she'd seen on George's lips. "I told the fellows you've been asking for it, you deaf and dumb bitch," he'd said.

She remembered the men looking her way at the dance, when George was talking to them. she thought of how she'd welcomed his kisses, his embraces, while all the while he'd been laughing at her, calling her deaf and dumb, telling his friends she was easy.

She'd allowed him liberties, believing his intentions were honorable. She felt sickened to think that perhaps she'd invited what had occurred.

She was a farm girl, she'd seen coupling between the animals, she knew that something similar occurred between people. Annie had explained to her once, when she asked, that when there was love between two people, sexual union was a joyful thing, a pleasure hard to even describe. Betsy had experimented, touching herself at night under the blankets, and she knew a little of what Annie meant.

She and Rose had spoken of sex, of what it felt like, of how it would happen after they were wed. Neither had ever imagined a scene such as this one with George Watson.

The more Betsy thought about it, the more ashamed she became. By the time the farmhouse was in view, she knew she couldn't say anything about what had happened. Shame was like a burning poison in her belly. Somehow, she'd made Watson think it was alright to treat her that way. It was because she was deaf. If she could hear, she'd have known what kind of man he really was.

She took the horses to the barn, unharnessed them, brushed and fed them. Bile rose in her throat and she vomited, heaving until there was nothing left in her stomach.

She slowly regained control. George slept in the barn, and she knew that he wouldn't be back anytime soon, nor, if her luck held, would Noah or Annie notice they hadn't returned together. She could see that Noah had already finished the evening chores. The cows were milked, the stalls cleaned, fresh hay spread.

She washed her face in the horse trough, and when she finally went in the house, Noah was helping Annie put the children to bed, and both were distracted enough with the youngsters not to notice anything amiss. She wished them all goodnight and hurried up to her room, and it was only after she was in bed that the full horror of what had happened finally overcame her. Shame burned like acid in her chest. She trembled so violently the bed shook, and she couldn't stop the river of tears that soaked her pillow.

She didn't sleep all night, and when dawn came, she was standing at the window when George crept out of the barn leading his horse, his belongings in a pack behind his saddle. He was leaving like a thief, sneaking away before the household stirred. He led the horse some distance and then rode at a trot along the lane and out of sight, and in a burst of rage and betrayal, Betsy wanted to lean out the window and scream invective at him. Of course she didn't. She couldn't. She'd never wished harder for speech, never regretted more her world of silence.

Noah and Annie were surprised and insulted that he hadn't so much as said goodbye to them. They quizzed

Betsy as to what had happened the night before, and she simply said they'd had a bad fight.

In the days that followed, Annie tried again and again to get Betsy to explain in detail what had occurred between her and George Watson, but Betsy would only say again that they'd quarreled, and that she was through with hearing men.

She'd stuck to that vow…..until now. She should have refused absolutely when James suggested seeing her again. Of course she'd have to see him again about the photograph he'd commissioned, but apart from that, she ought to have been more definite.

The trouble was, she wanted to see him again. Until she'd sat with him at Dunlap's, talking freely, laughing and enjoying a soda together as other couples were doing, she hadn't fully admitted to herself how solitary her life was here in the city.

Rose always insisted she come along on group outings, but after the first few times, Betsy usually declined. As she'd told James, people weren't comfortable around her. Now that Rose was courting with Philip, if Betsy tagged along she'd be—what was the word? Gooseberry. Rose had used it about a friend's brother who hung around when her friend wanted to be alone with her young man.

So what should she do about James's declaration that he was going to court her?

He hadn't even asked. He'd simply stated it as a fact.

She searched for the word that described that attitude. Arrogant. James Macleod was arrogant. Or maybe confident? Confident better described him. But she also knew he was honest.

And some traitorous part of her, certainly not her head, but her heart, had liked his confidence, his determined attitude. It was flattering to have him admire her.

At last, exhaustion claimed her and she felt herself slipping down into sleep. She was too tired tonight to make sense of anything. She'd have to deal with all of it in the morning.

When James returned to the barracks that evening, his staff sergeant, William Osler, was waiting for him. James's heart sank when he heard what Osler had to say. He'd been hoping against hope that he'd be in town for at least the next week. He wanted most urgently to see Betsy again as soon as possible—but it wasn't to be.

"There's been a murder in a railroad construction camp, and I want you to go and investigate, Macleod. Details are sketchy. The man who reported it is the victim's brother, name of Stone, Sidney Stone. He naturally claims his brother was innocent, murdered in cold blood. Apparently there was an altercation over a game of poker and Edmund Stone was shot. The workers are holding the man who did it prisoner until you can escort him back here. As you know, gambling and drinking are prohibited within a ten mile radius of the railroad line, so charges in that regard will be in order."

The brother was in the mess hall, crouched over a cup of cold coffee. Tear tracks painted clean lines through the imbedded grime on his face. "My only brother's dead," he burst out. "That som'a'bitch Dufrain murdered him in cold blood, claimed Ed was cheating. My brother ain't no cheat, sir. Now I'm gonna have to write to our Mama and tell her the awful news. It'll break her heart."

James expressed his condolences, then spent an hour trying to extract details of the shooting. The construction camp was about eight hours ride east of Medicine Hat.

Stone was determined to bring his brother's body back for a decent burial, and they left the following morning before dawn. Fortunately, the weather had cooled considerably. If it hadn't, the body would need to be buried at camp.

As the sky lightened and the first traces of pink heralded the sunrise, James thought again of his declaration to Betsy.

"I intend to court ye," he'd told her. He'd surprised himself by his declaration, but the more he thought about it, the more determined he became to win her over, convince her that her deafness and his hearing need not be a barrier between them. He'd take his time and slowly capture her heart. He'd signed up for five years with the mounted; he'd be a free man in another month, if he so chose. The government this very year had offered a grant of 160 acres of land to anyone settling on the prairies. James intended to apply.

Looking out over the rich, rolling grassland, James imagined building a substantial home, sowing wheat, raising livestock. Raising a family. He had money. His great uncle Rob Macleod, a bachelor and a miser, had left him a substantial amount in his will, and James hadn't touched it. It was wisely invested, and there'd be plenty to start a homestead when the time came. There'd be none of the stark hand-to-mouth existence that he'd seen more often than not among the new emigrants. He could afford to provide Betsy with anything her heart might desire, but he had to first convince her they were right together.

Stone was not a talkative man, and was obviously grieving for his brother, so James had plenty of time to think. He pondered on what type of house Betsy would like, what kind of barn he'd need, what type of wheat to plant.

He and Stone rode in silence much of the time, and Betsy was always present in his mind. His thoughts went to kissing her, making love to her. He'd been attracted to women before, and he'd enjoyed the favors of many, both in Canada and in Scotland. He'd never before met a woman he'd wanted to marry, however. It surprised him how suddenly and completely he'd known she was the one.

There was a connection between him and Betsy, a powerful physical attraction, certainly, but well beyond that, a mental connection that he'd never found before with a woman. He found her intelligent, challenging; her mind sharp and intuitive. Passionate, if her quickness to anger was any indication. Independent, certainly, which to him was a fine quality in a partner. Funny—he loved her humor.

He'd never be bored with her. If anything, her deafness added to the attraction. It allowed an element of privacy between them, a secret language they shared. It made her unique.

They stopped at midday. James had packed beans, bread, pemmican, and apples. It was a long and dusty ride, and the sun was sinking in the western sky by the time they rode into the construction camp.

The foreman of the camp, a dark-skinned giant named Higgenbottom, came rushing over. "I'm that sorry, but we lost him, sir. He got away. Dufrain had a knife hidden in his boot. In the night he cut the ropes and stabbed Freddy, what was guardin' him. He's crazy as a mad dog, Dufrain. Stole a horse and rode away. Freddy's in a bad way. Could you come and have a look at him, sir?"

James's heart sank. Instead of simply conducting a prisoner back to barracks, now he was going to have to try and track the reprobate, which could take weeks. He hurried after Higgenbottom, into one of the tents that made up the camp.

Freddy, a muscular, thin man, was lying on a camp cot, and one glance told James that the situation was serious. He was barely conscious, his breathing fast and uneven, his skin gray. James checked to make sure his airway was clear, and then drew back the rough brown blanket that covered him.

Blood was seeping out of the bandages wrapped clumsily around Freddy's chest.

James untied the grimy rags. The major entry wound was between the ribs, under the heart. If the knife had gone in at an upward angle as James suspected, chances were good that the vessels around the heart and perhaps the heart itself were damaged. There were two more entry wounds, one to the abdomen and one to the upper chest,

With a sinking feeling in his gut, James knew there was little he could do. The damage was lethal. Freddy would not survive, but he had to try. James called for a basin of hot water, soap, clean bandages, a bottle of whisky, all the while talking to the injured man, introducing himself, assuring him he'd do what he could to help, knowing all the while that there was really nothing to be done expect perhaps make the poor man more comfortable.

James took off his buckskin jacket, rolled up the sleeves of his shirt. When a small Chinese man brought the hot water and soap, he scrubbed his hands and arms. In a fresh basin he wet a rag and cleaned the wounds as best he could. The flow of blood made it difficult.

Freddy screamed, long and loud, and when the agonizing sound faded, the camp suddenly became silent, as if every man there felt death brush his shoulder.

Chapter Five

"Sorry, sorry, laddie," James muttered.

With deep puncture wounds like these, sepsis was almost inevitable, but chances were Freddy wouldn't survive long enough for infection to set in. James had no carbolic acid anyway, normally used to disinfect wounds and minimize germs. He filled a glass with whiskey and held it to the man's lips. There was nothing else available to try and ease the pain.

Moving his hand over Freddy's abdomen, he knew that blood was also rapidly filling the internal cavity, and by Freddy's torturous breathing, James suspected that the pleural cavity as well was compromised, and the lungs would soon collapse.

A terrible, familiar sense of hopelessness and frustration at his inability to help Freddy nearly choked him. James sat beside the injured man, talking to him quietly and wiping his sweat away with a cool cloth.

At three in the morning, Freddy died, calling for his mother and struggling to breathe, and up until the very last, in excruciating pain. The whiskey James had tried to administer dribbled out of his mouth. He couldn't seem to swallow.

James would have given anything to be able to ease the man's passing, and for the first time since leaving Scotland he cursed himself for his stubborn refusal to claim his status as a doctor.

Hidden in a storage locker back at the barracks he had a black Gladstone bag containing his medical supplies. Given to him by his grandfather when he graduated, he somehow hadn't been able to bring himself to throw what it contained away. In it were his prized surgical instruments in a rolled operating case, hypodermic needles, a few vials of morphine, and a small bottle of chloroform. He wished fervently that he'd had them with him tonight. Morphine would have meant the man died peacefully instead of in agony.

He washed Freddy's body, rolled it in a tightly bound blanket and secured it with light rope. The men had already prepared Edmund Stone's body in the same manner. Sidney and another man James deputized would transport both bodies back to Medicine Hat in the morning for a coroner's examination and then burial. He wrote a detailed report to be taken to the commanding officer at the detachment.

He then issued Higgenbottom with a cease-work order and a summons to appear in front of the magistrate for violation of the rule against gambling and drinking within a ten-mile radius of the railroad line. The man blustered, but James made certain he notified the crew of the closure. The men were subdued by the sight of the two wrapped bodies waiting to be loaded on horses in the morning, and they didn't argue.

James knew he'd have to leave again at daybreak in pursuit of the murderer, but sleep eluded him. He'd been given a tent and a cot, and as the long, dark hours passed, he lay in his bedroll and went over every detail of Freddy's death.

He knew he couldn't have saved him, but with his medical equipment at the ready, he also knew he could have eased the man's agony. Betsy's signed words came back to him as clearly as though she was in the tent beside him.

Doctor very good thing to be, she'd told him.

What would she think if she knew he was actually trained as a surgeon? Doctors were highly regarded in Scotland, but here on the Canadian prairies they were revered. There were far too few trained physicians, far too many charlatans who did more harm than healing.

How would he tell her the truth, how would he explain why he couldn't use his training? He wished now he'd been totally honest with her that first day, riding across the prairie. The longer he kept it secret, the harder it was going to be to explain. He had caused his sister's death, and tonight he hadn't been able to help Freddy.

But for the first time since leaving Scotland, he saw the total denial of his medical training as a senseless, selfish act, an act of cowardice, and he was ashamed. But he wasn't certain, either, that he could overcome his lack of confidence in himself enough to take up the practice of medicine again. His sister's death had broken something in him, and he didn't know how to mend it.

He got up an hour before dawn, filled a basin and washed himself. The cold water was bracing, and the hot, bitter coffee the cook provided very welcome. He ate a bowl of oatmeal from the huge pot that had been slowly cooking all night over the banked campfire at the cookhouse, and he wrote two notes, one to Staff Sergeant Osler apprising him of the situation and asking him to send a native tracker to assist him in finding the murderer.

The other note was to Betsy.

He gave both letters to the deputy, with instructions to deliver Betsy's note to Mrs. Coleman's boarding house.

One of the men had told James that Dufrain was from Montana. He had family there, and the man figured that's where the murderer would likely be headed, but he had no idea where Dufrain's family might be located. Montana was a huge territory.

As soon as the first streaks of dawn showed in the eastern sky, James saddled Ajax and rode toward the border.

The morning after James's proclamation, Betsy was already in the dining room having breakfast when Rose came bouncing down the stairs. She winked at Betsy, and then filled her plate with eggs, bacon and biscuits before taking her place at the table, waiting until Aunt Harriet had gone back in the kitchen to refill the coffee urn before confronting Betsy.

"Tell all right now, I'm dying to know," she signed forcefully. "Your James is a pip. Is he bringing you to the social on Friday?"

Betsy shook her head, wishing she could control the blush that washed over her face. "Not my James," she signed. "Just policeman that Noah asked to bring me home."

Rose rolled her eyes and blew a raspberry. "I saw the way he looked at you. He's smitten. You were walking out with him, Bets."

Suddenly Betsy longed to talk over the entire James situation with her friend, but just then Aunt Harriet bustled back into the dining room, pouring the girls coffee and then filling her own cup. "I'm that pleased ye've found yerself a fine wee Scots laddie, Betsy," she said. "Ye're James is a braw fella, to be sure."

She shot the young women a puzzled glance when they both burst into helpless giggles.

"I was just telling her the identical same thing," Rose explained, glancing at the wall clock and hurriedly finishing her food. "I'm late," she told them, signing to Betsy, "Tonight, you shall tell all, you vixen. I'll meet you after work." She carried her plate and utensils to the kitchen and waved goodbye, hurrying out the door.

Betsy finished her toast and coffee, making conversation with Aunt Harriet about the weather, praying the subject of James wouldn't come up again. She didn't want to discuss him until she knew exactly what she was going to do about him. A the moment, she had no idea whatsoever.

The day passed quickly. From the moment Betsy arrived at Miss Evangaline's Dressmaking Emporium, she was kept busy hemming, taking in, letting out, mending tears, doing beading. She wasn't an accomplished dressmaker, but she was excellent at alteration.

She worked in a stuffy little back room, but she didn't mind at all. The job paid her enough to afford her the modest board and room Rose's Aunt Harriet charged and, with the money she made from the photos she took, she was able to put a substantial amount away for her dream— her own photographic studio.

It also gave her much time to think, she decided, fingers busy with the difficult task of hemming a satin dress cut on the bias. Her injured wrist made the task difficult, but she found if she took her time, she could manage. Maybe she had too much time to think, because she couldn't get James out of her head.

Rose was waiting for her when the day was over, sitting on the chaise longue that Miss Evangeline had placed in an alcove of the shop.

"I've got some cream buns, let's go sit by the river," Rose suggested, and Betsy nodded with enthusiasm. One of her favorite places in the town was a small park by the South Saskatchewan River. There were wooden benches situated under the cottonwood trees, overlooking the water, and on sweltering late autumn days like this one, it was cool and pleasant to stroll and then sit and watch the river flow by.

Today, however, Rose had more on her mind than just sitting observing the water and wolfing cream buns. She handed Betsy one, and the moment they'd swallowed their last bite, her nimble fingers were flying. She wanted to know everything about James.

"How did he learn to sign? How old is he? How long has he been with the North-West Mounted? What did you two talk about? He has the most enchanting Scots accent, can you tell by lip-reading him?"

The barrage of demands made Betsy laugh. "Slow," she commanded. "I have two hands, one not working great."

"Sorry, sorry," Rose apologized, and then immediately asked all the questions again.

One by one, Betsy answered them.

"When are you seeing him again?" Rose wanted to know.

Betsy shrugged. "Has to come for photograph, maybe tomorrow or next day."

"You do like him fine, don't you, Betsy? You'd have to be loonie not to, he's perfect for you."

Betsy shook her head. "Hearing man, deaf woman, not good."

Rose blew a raspberry. "How do you know if you don't try? For land's sake, Betsy, just because that sap of a George Watson was a no-good louse."

Rose was the only one Betsy had confided in about what Watson had really done.

"You know what my mother always says," Rose went on. "If at first you don't succeed, try, try again. You do fancy him, don't you?"

Betsy had to nod, and she felt a blush rise up her face. Fancy was a mild word for the feelings James aroused in her.

"Well, there you have it. He's smitten with you, I saw the way he looks at you."

"He says he wants to court me," Betsy admitted.

"Hooray!" Rose leaped to her feet and danced around in a circle, drawing disapproving looks from an older couple walking sedately along the river path. "Oh, Betsy, it's perfect, we can have a double wedding, we'll have Miss Evangeline make our dresses and Gunderson's will bake us an enormous cake, and......."

Betsy took her friend's hands in hers, stilling the flying fingers, shaking her head. "Maybe he gets tired of sign, sign, all the time. Maybe after time he wants hearing woman like him."

"Balderdash. Do I ever get tired of signing?"

Betsy thought that over. She shook her head. "You are my heart friend," she said. "Like sisters, love each other."

"So why shouldn't it be the same with James? Married people can be friends, look at Annie and Noah. They love each other, and they're also friends."

Again, Rose's logic made it hard to argue, but Betsy had been thinking of every eventuality. "I want very much studio, take photographs. Married, not possible."

That subdued Rose. They both knew it was rare for a woman to have a career unless she was a spinster. The demands of housekeeping and motherhood alone made it well neigh impossible, and most men objected to their wives working. It was a matter of pride and ego. Many men felt it made them look as if they couldn't support their families.

"Did you tell him that when he said he wanted to court you?"

Betsy shook her head.

"Well then, you silly goose, tell him. He's obviously an intelligent man, perhaps he'll have a solution."

But as they walked home, Betsy couldn't think what it might be.

In spite of her reservations, during the following day and the day after that Betsy found herself waiting for James. She developed the photos she'd taken, marveling at how handsome he was. She had frames she'd made, and she mounted and framed several. She also kept one for herself, guiltily tucking it under her pantaloons in the dresser drawer.

On Thursday afternoon, from her bedroom window, she caught a glimpse of a red tunic coming down the garden walk toward the house, and her heart started to hammer. She tucked stubborn curls back into her bun, checked her face in the mirror and then frantically brushed pieces of thread off of her dark work skirt before hurrying downstairs.

Miss Harriet was just closing the door. She held an envelope which she extended to Betsy. "A policeman brought this for ye just this wee minute, darlin'. Said it was from yer James Macleod."

Betsy took the envelope, her hands trembling. She knew he was writing to say he'd changed his mind. He wasn't even courageous enough to come and tell her in person. She thanked her landlady and went hurrying up the stairs, closing the door of her room and sinking down on the bed before she could bring herself to rip the envelope open and unfold the single sheet.

Her heart hammered as if it would pound its way out of her chest, and bitter disappointment made her stomach feel sick. A sob bubbled up. She drew in a breath and held it, and then forced herself to unfold the sheet and read it.

My dear Betsy,

Urgent police matters prevent me from keeping my assignation with you this week, but I'm hopeful to be back in a week or two. Unfortunately I'm unable to judge the length of my absence with any accuracy and beg for your patience. I shall think of you fondly and constantly, and hope so very much that you have reconsidered your position on courtship. If I could give up my hearing to win you, dear Betsy, I would do so without a single regret.

Yours,
James R. Macleod.

She blew out her breath and read it through twice and then again, scarcely able to take in the full meaning. She could hardly believe he would write such a forthright, affectionate letter to her. His honesty and concern that she know why he couldn't keep his word touched her heart. The final sentence, about giving up his hearing, brought another sob to her throat.

She threw herself back on her bed, holding the note to her heart. She couldn't deny the powerful feelings James aroused in her, despite her resolution not to be courted by him. A tightly coiled skein of stubbornness and doubt began to unravel in her.

Perhaps she needed to pay attention to what Annie and Rose kept saying, that she was foolish to exclude hearing men when it came to romance. Maybe it was time to trust again, to get to know James better, to find out whether or not their relationship might work in spite of their differences.

She would have time to consider it before she saw him again. From the letter it sounded as if his mission might be a long one, and she felt a sharp pang of regret. She wished he was here now to talk to, to express what she was feeling. Obviously there was no way to send a note back to him, wherever he was.

She wondered where exactly, and what he was doing. She sent a silent, fervent prayer to the heavens that he be kept safe and come back unharmed.

Chapter Six

The Indian tracker James had requested joined him on the third day after leaving the railroad camp.

James had lost Dufrain's trail that afternoon, but the tracker, Black Eagle, picked it up again the following morning. Dufrain's horse had only been partially shod, and Black Eagle followed the tracks easily, even though wily Dufrain had waded for some distance in a stream.

A Blood Indian, Black Eagle had spent time in jail for allegedly killing a Mountie. When he was released, he became one of the force's best trackers. Bedded down beside the taciturn Indian during the long cool nights, listening to the coyotes howl, James could only hope that the man's penchant for murdering Mounties was specific rather than general.

At first, Black Eagle's English seemed basic at best, so spoken communication was limited. James used some basic signs, and the Indian taught him some of his own, but it wasn't until the third day on the trail that James realized the other man actually had an excellent command of English.

"Why did ye not talk with me at first?" he asked, annoyed when he found out Black Eagle was fluent in English. "Ye made a bloody fool outa me, man."

"Learn more by listening. White man talks to himself or his friends, thinks Indian can't understand, so he says what he is really thinking. No lies. I hear the truth."

"Where did ye learn the Queen's English, ye devious scoundrel?"

"Jail. There is much to be learned in white man's jail."

James laughed. He'd never thought of prison as being an educational opportunity. "I heard ye were there fer murder." James wanted to hear Black Eagle's version of the sentence. "Why did ye see fit to shoot the Mountie?"

Black Eagle took his time answering. "Bad man. Lies with small girl instead of squaw. My sister's girl. Five summers." He held out a hand, five fingers extended. "Hurt her."

James digested that, his gorge rising as the full impact of Black Eagle's words became clear to him. "Shooting was too good for the bastard. He needed his bollocks sliced off."

Black Eagle nodded, and something in his expression convinced James that that was exactly what had occurred...doubtless before the shooting. He tried not to visualize it, although he knew it to be just.

"Why did the judge send ye to jail? Did he no understand what had happened?" He should have given

Black Eagle a medal instead of a jail sentence, in James's estimation.

Black Eagle pointed a finger at James. "White man," he said. He turned the finger toward his own chest. "Indian."

James swore. He knew Black Eagle was right. There were many in the Force who treated the Indians with fairness, but there also some who did not, seeing no further than the color of their skin. But on the other hand, many magistrates would have sentenced him to hang. Black Eagle had managed to appear before a man who at least took the circumstances into account.

"Are ye wed?" Betsy was never far from his mind, and his own aspirations for family piqued his interest in what other men did in that regard.

It seemed Black Eagle had two wives, four sons, and a newly married daughter, who was about to make him a grandfather. His own grandfather was Big Bear, a famous chief.

Each night when they made camp, Black Eagle told James a little more about his people, how they were slowly losing their hunting grounds and their nomadic way of life, and James related stories about growing up in Scotland. Black Eagle was particularly interested in James's tales of the Loch Ness monster. He asked James to tell the story again and again.

"You were Mountie in Scotland?"

James shook his head. then to his own amazement, he told the other man about being a doctor, adding only that he wasn't one anymore.

Black Eagle gave him an inscrutable look. "You made strong medicine?"

James thought about that and nodded. "I was a good doctor, yes." Until he wasn't.

"Medicine man is always medicine man," the Indian grunted. "Like being Chief, not something a man stops being." He immediately returned to Nessie and Loch Ness. "You have seen this monster yourself?"

"No, but my brother did." With a sigh, James went back to the topic that fascinated Black Eagle. So much for deep discussions about emotional matters.

But the next night Black Eagle asked why James had given up medicine.

And James found himself, for the first time, telling the whole story. There was something about Black Eagle that made telling the truth not only easy, but also imperative. He listened in silence, not judging or commenting.

James began with the years at Edinburgh University, his training as a surgeon, his desire to stay in Edinburgh after his graduation.

"We had only the one old doctor in our village, Allen Mcfee, who needed to retire. So I did as my father asked and went back home to take over Mcfee's practice." That part was easy enough to relate. It was the next that he'd never talked about, and wasn't certain he could now.

Black Eagle put wood on the campfire and waited silently, and at last James cleared his throat and went on.

"My mother had lost children. My youngest brother, Simon, died when he was five of a fever, and she miscarried two baby girls before she had my wee sister, Marguerite. All of us doted on her, and my mother and father adored her." James swallowed hard, thinking of his baby sister. "She was a lovely lass, inside and out. She grew into a bonny young woman, and married young, she was but sixteen. She'd fallen in love with Brian Stewart, son of my father's best friend. She fell pregnant right away, and the birth was eagerly awaited. The Stewart clan had no immediate male heirs, so a boy was hoped for, and my mother longed for a grandbaby, lass or lassie made no difference."

The next part of the story was torment to recall. "Marguerite's labor began a month early, in the middle of the night, in a storm. I was called and I sent a groom immediately to fetch Mcfee. There was something seriously wrong. Marguerite had a severe headache and was running a high fever, and I suspected a condition called eclampsia."

He appreciated that Black Eagle didn't interrupt or ask questions, even though James knew some of the medical terms would probably sound like gibberish to Black Eagle. He was paying close attention, however.

The memories of that terrible night rolled over James

in waves of agony, and he could feel the burning of unshed tears in his throat and behind his eyes. The quail they'd roasted for dinner no longer rested easy in his belly.

"Mcfee arrived, and I told him what I suspected. Marguerite was having convulsions by then, and I felt the only chance of saving her and the child was a surgical procedure called caesarian section."

He explained as well as he could. "It's when a woman can nae deliver her baby, and her life is in danger. The surgeon opens her abdomen wi' a blade and takes the baby out."

Black Eagle was impressed. "This is possible? Baby lives? Mother lives?"

James shrugged. "It's a risky operation, I'd only seen it performed successfully once. Mcfee had never seen it done, and he disagreed strongly, insisting we let nature take its course. My father and Brian were called in to make a decision, and they sided with me." He swallowed hard. The familiar overwhelming sense of terrible guilt and black despair nearly choked him.

"Mcfee was furious, but he agreed to assist me." James's throat closed, and he had to clear it several times before he could continue. Part of him wondered why it was imperative right now to talk about this. He hadn't told anyone else in Canada. Why should he feel compelled to tell Black Eagle? But whatever the reason, he had to continue now that he'd begun.

"Marguerite--she convulsed as I was performing the surgery. The scalpel slipped and I severed an artery. She died in moments, and I tried to save the child, a wee boy. But he was too small to breathe, and he, too, died within the hour."

Black Eagle was silent and James didn't look at him. He hurriedly finished the story, his voice thick with emotion.

"Mcfee convinced everyone I'd murdered my sister. He insisted that if I'd followed his advice, Marguerite and the baby would have lived. I couldn't be certain he was wrong. I could nae go on being a surgeon because of it. As soon as the funeral was over, I signed on with the North-West Mounted and came to Canada."

He skipped the ugly details of the inquest, the formal accusations Mcfee had made, charging him with incompetence. He'd realized too late the old doctor resented him, resented his modern ideas.

He'd been acquitted in a court of law, but nothing could ease the grief, the overwhelming guilt and pain of knowing members of his family and especially the Stewarts must wonder in their hearts if what Mcfee claimed was true, that Marguerite and the child might have lived without his surgical intervention. None of them had ever said as much or even hinted it, but James couldn't stand to be around them. He imagined blame whether it was there or not, because he blamed himself.

"When a man falls from a horse, he must get on that horse and ride him again," Black Eagle said, filling his cup with coffee from the pot on the fire.

James knew it was good advice. He just wasn't certain he could apply it.

They lost the trail entirely somewhere in Montana, so James headed for an American post, Fort Shaw, hoping the policemen there might know of Dufrain or his family, and fortunately one of the constables stationed there had once arrested Dufrain for smuggling whiskey. Before he could be brought on charges, he'd escaped across the border. The constable thought he was from a tiny settlement to the east, so James and Black Eagle set out to find it.

James had now been away from Medicine Hat for twelve days, and he hoped Betsy had received the note he'd sent her. She was constantly on his mind. He was weary of living rough on the trail. The weather had changed, and it rained constantly. His boots and clothing were always damp from the storms and from fording rivers. Food was limited to what he and Black Eagle could shoot or catch in addition to the hard tack and pemmican they carried.

As the long, tedious days of riding dragged past, James became more and more determined to change his way of life. Like nothing else, this trip was proving to him that he'd had enough of the adventure the North-West

Mounted provided. As his thirty-fifth birthday drew near, he determined to take his leave of the Mounted once this hellish trip was over.

During the long nights he stared up at the starlit sky, imagining what a settled life might be like with Betsy, thinking eagerly of the children they'd have, planning in his mind every detail of the house he'd build them. All, of course, dependent on whether or not he could win her hand and her heart.

He thought as well about what he'd do once he left the force. His mind still shied away from the practice of medicine. He'd farm, he decided, grow wheat, raise animals. Cattle: he'd go into cattle. He'd have a ranch instead of a farm, he revised. His father had thousands of head of cattle. James had grown up the son of a laird who was involved always in livestock and farming, and he knew well how to manage such a business.

He was going to have to tell Betsy why he'd left Scotland, though. He ought to have told her on their long ride across the prairie. He was sorry now he hadn't.

On the afternoon of the sixteenth day, they reached the settlement the constable had described. The few residents were unfriendly and surly when he inquired after Dufrain, and James thought most of them were probably his relatives. If the wanted man was here, he could be hiding anywhere in the vicinity, and finding him was going to be next to impossible if no one would talk.

There were a few natives camped outside the settlement, and Black Eagle disappeared with them for a few hours. When he returned he beckoned to James to follow him, indicating that he'd located Dufrain's camp. They rode away from the ramshackle hovels, into the trees that bordered a river. After about a mile, Black Eagle dismounted. James did as well, and they tethered the horses, and then set out on foot, Black Eagle indicating the need for silence.

They crept through the brush beside a creek, and then Black Eagle crouched and indicated a tent and the remains of a campfire. The camp was well hidden in heavy brush.

"We wait," Black Eagle signed, squatting down on his heels.

The camp looked deserted, and after watching for over an hour with no sign of anyone, James stood, holding his Colt revolver at the ready.

Black Eagle shook his head, making a sign for wait, but James had had enough of waiting. With Black Eagle covering his back, James walked over to the tent, cautiously pulling the flap aside. It was empty, but as he straightened and half turned, he thought someone hit him in the head with something heavy. He didn't hear the sound of the first shot, but he heard the second, aware of burning pain in his thigh as he fell to the ground, and just before he lost consciousness, he thought he heard one more shot fired—then, darkness.

Chapter Seven

James came to for brief periods, taking several moments each time to figure out what was happening to him. The first time, he was laced to a travois, being roughly dragged behind a horse, and he wanted only to die from the overwhelming pain in his head and in his leg. Every jolt was agonizing. He gagged and turned his head to vomit, but he couldn't summon enough strength or breath even to protest, and it was a relief to lose consciousness again.

The next time he woke there was an old Indian woman in a buckskin dress staring down at him. He realized he was naked, shuddering from cold. He was looking up at the center poles in a teepee. She bent down and put something on the wound on his thigh, something that hurt like fury, and he heard a scream of someone in agony. Merciful blackness again.

The next time he came out of the unfathomable darkness he was burning with fever. A younger Indian woman forced his mouth open and dribbled bitter, slimy liquid on his tongue. He gagged and then swallowed, and she held a cup to his lips, indicating that he should drink. He did, and the potion made him gag again, it was so foul. She pinched his nostrils shut until he had to swallow. She insisted he drink more, and too weak to protest, he tried and then choked. She waited patiently and then held the cup to his lips forcefully. This time he swallowed the horrible concoction just so she'd leave him alone.

He came out of unconsciousness again with no idea how much time he'd been senseless. This time he stayed awake longer, groggily becoming aware of the smoky teepee, the smell of the pungent bear hides under him, the fire a few feet away. He was still naked, wrapped in a rough wool blanket, with a bear hide blanket over that. He desperately wanted the coverings off, because he was fiery hot and sweating, but he hadn't the strength to move them. The woman who'd fed him the bitter liquid was there and she peeled them back, however, and James let out a howl as she removed a dressing of leaves from his wound, applied salve that burned like fire, and then replaced fresh leaves that she was using as a dressing, propping his injured leg on a rolled blanket.

She replaced the other coverings and left, and a few moments later Black Eagle came into the tepee. He sat down cross-legged a few feet from James, and explained that Dufrain had been hiding in a tree, and had shot James, not once, but twice. One bullet had grazed the back of his head, the other had gone in one side of his thigh and out the other. Black Eagle had shot Dufrain.

"Dead?" James inquired, having to try several times to get the single word past the dryness in his throat. His voice was trembly and weak.

Black Eagle nodded impassively, and used his hands in a graphic pantomime, showing how Dufrain had tumbled down from the tree and lain dead on the ground.

"Good," James mumbled. "Thank you." He cleared his throat again and croaked, "You saved my life. Where exactly are we?"

"Montana. Some of my people live here."

"I have to get back to Medicine Hat."

"Not this day," Black Eagle said with a cheerful grin. "You aren't dead, but you're not so good for riding a horse."

It was obvious he was right. James couldn't even sit up by himself, much less mount a horse. He'd had to be hauled outside by two strong squaws each time he needed to empty his bladder or bowels, a humiliating experience if ever there was one, particularly because the women laughed uproariously and although he couldn't be absolutely sure, made comments to one another on the size of his privates.

James smiled weakly at Black Eagle, assessed how he felt and regretfully shook his head, which hurt so much he groaned. "You're right," he finally managed. "I cannae ride yet. Maybe in one or two days?"

That optimistic outlook made Black Eagle laugh uproariously and shake his head. "Always in a hurry, white man." He held up ten fingers, indicating how long he thought it would be before James could ride a horse. "Maybe."

James asked how many days since he'd been shot, and Black Eagle held up five fingers. James then spent a long time figuring out how long he'd been away. In all, it must be over four weeks since he'd left Medicine Hat. He figured it was now October. He thought of Betsy and hoped that she'd gotten his note. He desperately wanted to get back to her. This brush with death had solidified his intention to change his way of life. If he lived through it.

After Black Eagle and the young woman left, James struggled to sit up. He needed to know the exact extent of his injuries.

Gritting his teeth against the pain in his leg and the sledgehammer pounding in his head, he removed the herbs and leaves that covered the thigh wound, and tried to determine the full extent of the damage. The bullet had entered at a downward angle, going straight through his thigh midway between his knee and his groin. The jagged wound was red and angry, but not seriously infected that he could see. There was no pus, and none of the putrid smell which would signal gangrene. It hurt like the devil, however. Next, he felt the back of his head with his hand. The bullet had carved a deep furrow in his scalp. The wound was covered in something greasy, but it too, seemed to be healing, although the excruciating pain in his head didn't indicate that.

He was feverish, which could mean a degree of infection, but the bullet in his thigh must have passed through the soft flesh and exited. If it had lodged inside, or shattered the bone, he'd probably be dead already from infection. Whatever the Indians had done was working. He struggled to stay sitting up, but the pain was enormous and he was weak. He replaced the mess of leaves on his thigh and sank back into the blanket cocoon, and down into sleep.

Since she'd gotten the note from James, Betsy had spent every day waiting expectantly for his return. But six weeks had passed, and she was losing hope. The weather was still good, cold at night and sunny in the day, but it was only a matter of time before winter storms began. If he didn't make it back before then, travel would be difficult, if not impossible. Where was he?

The only thing that took her mind off of James was her camera. She walked around the city with her Pocket Zar, capturing images of buildings, of people's faces, of children playing. It was slow, because she could take only one photo on each excursion. She wandered by the river, taking photos of the trees and the water. Twice she rescued

Jingles from the livery and rode along the river. She felt too unsettled to make the long journey home, but she saw Noah and the boys twice, when they came in for supplies. Annie was feeling fine, Noah reported. Betsy wrote notes for Annie, but it was to Rose she confided her worst fears.

"Something bad happened to James, too long away now," she told Rose as they walked home from work one afternoon in mid-October. They both wore warm shawls over their coats; the weather had turned cool and rainy. "Maybe dead, nobody would tell me if police heard." Putting her worst fears into words made her stomach sick.

"We should simply go to the barracks and ask," practical Rose signed. "Let's do that, right now. It's not too far a walk, and the rain has stopped. Better to know for sure than to be kept in limbo this way."

"They will think we are fallen angels." Rose had explained about women who sold their bodies. Betsy had been shocked and fascinated.

Rose blew a raspberry. "Who cares what they think? You need to know instead of fretting this way."

It took them more than half an hour to reach the police barracks, and Betsy would have lost her nerve if Rose hadn't marched them straight past all the uniformed men who stared at them curiously. Rose asked a man grooming a horse where the commanding officer was, and one of the Mounties led them to a long wooden building. He took them to an office that had been partitioned off and knocked on the door, then stepped aside to allow them to enter.

The officer sitting at a desk sprang to his feet, bowed to them, and gestured that they should sit. "Staff Sergeant Osler at your service, ladies. What can I do for you?"

Betsy watched as Rose introduced them both, using speech and sign. Her own hands were trembling, and she hid them in her skirt.

Rose said, "We are acquaintances of Sergeant James Macleod. He is a friend of Miss Ferguson's brother-in-law. Would it be possible to speak to the Sergeant? We would like to invite him to a social gathering."

They'd discussed what they would say, and that had seemed the most reasonable.

Betsy watched closely as Osler answered, desperately trying to lip read, terrified that he was going to say James was dead. Unfortunately, he had a full moustache, which made it difficult. Why did men insist on wearing those stupid things? Her heart was hammering, and she felt hot and then cold, her stomach cramping.

Rose's fingers flew as she interpreted what Osler said.

"Sergeant Macleod—injured in the course of duty—arrived at the infirmary three days ago—gunshot to his leg, wound to the head."

Betsy clamped a hand over her mouth, and Rose reached over and patted her arm.

"---in the infirmary—you can see him there----"

Betsy's knees were shaking, and it was hard to stand up.

Osler took them himself, along a wooden walkway and into a room equipped as a surgery. Another doorway led to a small room, scrupulously clean but bare except for a narrow bed, a single chair, and a small stove in one corner. The man asleep in the bed was James, but Betsy couldn't prevent the shocked sound she made when she first saw him.

James was pale and gaunt, the wide white bandage around his head nearly the same color as his skin. He had an unkempt beard, and his skin was shiny with sweat. There were dark hollows underneath his eyes. He'd lost an alarming amount of weight, and his cheekbones stood out in harsh relief. He wore a loose blue nightshirt, and the rough gray blankets were held up off his legs by a tent-like apparatus.

Osler laid a gentle hand on James's shoulder, and he must also have said something, because James woke up with a start. He frowned up at Osler, confused, and then he saw Betsy. His face lit up, and he struggled to sit up.

"Betsy."

Osler gently pressed him back on the pillows, saying something to Rose.

"He says James is weak, we can only stay a few moments, he needs to rest," she signed to Betsy.

Betsy moved closer to James, longing to touch him,

too aware of Osler and Rose close behind her. "I am so sorry you are hurt," she told him. "Is there anything we can bring for you?" Seeing him so weak and obviously ill made something in her chest ache. She struggled to hold back the tears that burned behind her eyes.

"I apologize for the beard. If you promise to come see me soon again, I'll shave and make meself presentable." His hand trembled as he signed, but he smiled at her, and his eyes locked on hers. The intensity of his gaze seemed to convey something quite different than his signed words. "I am so very pleased to see ye, Betsy, thank you for coming." He added after a moment, "And you too, Miss Rose," but it was obviously an afterthought.

The girls made polite conversation for a few moments, but it was obvious that James was struggling. He was pasty white, and sweat stood out on his forehead. He had only one pillow, and propping himself up on an elbow so he could sign obviously drained him.

Osler indicated that they should leave, and he escorted them out. As the other two reached the door, Betsy turned back and signed quickly, "I will come soon again, please rest, get well quickly."

And then, with Rose and Osler safely out of sight, James made urgent signs that took her breath away. He looked straight into her eyes and signed, "I love you, Betsy, I want you to know that," and then he lay back, panting and exhausted, and closed his eyes.

On the walk back to town, Rose said with a wide grin, "He's so sweet on you, Bets. It was plain as the nose on your face, he barely even knew I was there. Don't try and tell me you don't feel the same way, I saw your expression when you first saw him."

Betsy, still overwhelmed by James's condition and his declaration of love, didn't bother to deny Rose's words. "He looks very bad," she told Rose. She felt sick with worry. "Very weak, very sick." She swiped at her eyes, wiping the tears on her sleeve. She'd had to struggle to keep from touching him, wiping the sweat off his forehead, getting him to drink something.

"I have an idea about that," Rose said with a little skip. "Auntie likes him a lot, and he's a fellow Scot. She's a good nurse, and you know how she loves to fuss. I'll bet she'll sort it out when we tell her about that bare room and the one pillow. Those rough blankets, we mustn't forget those."

"Why, the poor wee Scots laddie, lyin' there all alone wi' only rough men ta tend him," Aunt Harriet humphed when Rose told her at dinner that evening about their visit to the detachment. "He needs proper nursin' and good solid food if he's tae get well again. He needs a woman's care. I'll just pay yon Osler mannie a visit in the morning, and see what we can do about this."

Rose winked at Betsy. "What did I tell you?"

Chapter Eight

Sure enough, by the time Betsy and Rose got home from work the following day, the door was open to the downstairs parlor and a cheerful fire burned in the grate. A bed had been set up, and James, shaved and wearing a fresh white shirt and a kilt, lay in gleaming white sheets propped on three thick goose feather pillows, already looking better than he had the day before.

Betsy, remembering what he'd said to her, was suddenly shy, and started toward the stairs to go to her room. Rose grabbed her arm, though, and dragged her over to James's bed.

After the first polite greetings, Rose said, "So did Auntie Hannah kidnap you, Sergeant?"

"I, that she did," James said, talking to Rose but looking at Betsy. "Before I knew what was happening, she'd bullied Staff into loading me in a wagon and bringing me here. I have to say, I didn't much protest. This is far preferable to the infirmary."

Rose pushed Betsy into a chair and took the other one

herself.

"Now," she signed, "You absolutely must tell us how you got shot. Every single detail," she demanded. "We are simply dying to know."

James had considered refusing when Ostler told him that Mrs. Coleman was insisting he be moved to her house to recuperate. He hated being an invalid, resented not being able to walk more than a few steps. He could barely contain his temper when the police surgeon insisted he needed full bed rest in order to recover movement in his leg. The long ride from the Indian camp had weakened him, and he'd developed a fever again.

He'd barked at the poor man, and was short-tempered with the constable assigned to the infirmary. James knew he was a terrible patient, and he didn't want to inflict himself on anyone. Besides that, he loathed being seen in his bed shirt, and he was still not able to wear the tight fitting trousers to his uniform. His thigh was swollen to twice its size. Black Eagle had supplied him with a pair of loose buckskin pants for the excruciating ride back to the detachment, and he'd been pathetically grateful for those pants until he was able to unearth his kilt from his locker and wrap it around him.

But moving to Harriet's house meant that he'd see Betsy, and he wanted that more than anything. So he'd agreed, insisting first on a bath and a shave, which had been no mean feat. He'd come near to passing out and, angered by his weakness, he'd bitten the head off the poor boy who'd assisted him. The lad had no idea whatsoever how a kilt was meant to be worn.

Now he was determined to curb his temper and exercise his leg every day in spite of the surgeon's dire warnings about infection and permanent damage if he didn't stay off it. He had every intention of getting his strength back and being back on his feet within a few days. Well, perhaps a week, but no more than that. The long, wet ride back to the detachment from Montana had taken its toll, and he was still exhausted.

But he had a crutch by his bedside, and he'd already managed the trip out the back door to the outhouse. Harriet, bless her kind Scots soul, had washed and ironed a fresh shirt for him, so at least he wasn't half-dressed at the moment.

Trying not to stare at Betsy, who was breathtakingly lovely in a lilac-patterned dress that skimmed over her breasts and emphasized her narrow waist, he made short work of explaining how he'd been stupid enough to get himself shot.

"When we reached Dufrene's camp, Black Eagle told me to keep still and wait, but I was impatient. I'm surprised he took the trouble to drag me back to his people afterwards. He made it clear I was an impulsive fool. It took me a wee while before I could ride, so we stayed in the Indian camp."

He skipped over the agonizing ride back to barracks, emphasizing instead the kindness and care he'd had from the Indians.

"What's it like in their camp?" Rose wanted to know. "They used to come to the farm sometimes. They'd come in the house and sit around forever until mom fed them."

"Same at our farm," Betsy agreed. "Always they came back later, brought us gifts like venison, baskets, once a honeycomb."

"They took good care of me," James said. "They used herbal medicines, they seemed to know how to counteract infection." They'd also hauled him up and forced him to move around, in direct contrast to the bed rest the police surgeon insisted on. In spite of the agony moving had caused him, James thought the Indian's method was better. It made sense that movement brought blood into the area and probably helped with healing. He was fascinated by the herbal concoctions they'd used, and once he was well again he planned to study them.

But right at this moment, he only had eyes for Betsy. She was sitting in the armchair a few feet away from his bed, her lilac skirt smoothed modestly over knees and ankles, the color setting off her golden skin and coppery hair. Her elegant hands were folded in her lap as she watched his signs, and her mobile features reflected her sympathetic reactions to his story. He loved the sprinkling of freckles across her nose, and the way her mobile face mirrored her emotions.

He was prattling on about Black Eagle, but he wished desperately that he could speak to her alone. He felt a great urgency now that he was near her, needing to tell her what was in his heart, wanting to know her reaction. Every day made him more and more determined and impatient to get on with his life—their life--and he wanted nothing more than to convey his feelings to Betsy and somehow convince her to let him court her, marry her.

Rose was perceptive. The moment James finished his story, she got to her feet.

"You must excuse me, it's my night to help Auntie with dinner. You stay here, Bets, and entertain the sergeant. I'm sure he's bored to death and needs someone to talk to." She half-closed the parlor door—closing it completely would be a scandalizing breach of etiquette. Then she hurried away.

At last, at last, they were alone.

James had been reclining on the bed, his injured leg propped up on pillows. Now he sat up and swung both legs off the side, ignoring the bolt of pain it caused. He wanted to at least be sitting up while he spoke to her. He longed to take her in his arms, show her with his body's language how he felt, but he remembered all too well her reaction to having him close to her. He needed to heed

Black Eagle's comment about white men always being in a hurry.

Her gaze skimmed over his kilt, took in his bare legs, and he saw her swallow. Obviously the lass had never seen a man in Highland dress before. All the more reason to not rush her.

Go slow, Macleod, go slow. Patience, lad.

Before he could begin to say anything Betsy's hands flew, and his good intentions disappeared like smoke.

"You say you love me. You mean that?" A blush turned her skin pink, but she met his gaze without faltering, and he was amazed at her bravery, her forthright manner.

"With all my heart, Betsy. I want us to get to know one another better, I want ye to come to love me. More than anything in this world, I want ye to marry me. Do I have even a ghost of a chance?"

His heart raced as he waited for her answer. She was very still for several moments, and then she began signing rapidly and with passion.

"Yes. I have big feelings for you also, but I have plan for my life. I want to be photographer, have studio, my own business. Be free. I want this since I was young girl. Not possible if married."

"I don't see why not," he responded. "I would support you in every way I could. I have no objection to a woman having a career of her own. One of my cousins, Jennie, is a doctor. She's married, her husband Stewart is a businessman in Edinburgh. He moved there so she could work at the University Hospital."

Betsy was beyond surprised at that. "Doctor? Woman doctor?" She shook her open hand up and down in the sign for admiration and amazement. "She has children?"

He nodded, feeling a sharp pang of guilt at deceiving her about his own medical training. "Children, yes." He held up three fingers. "They have a nannie and a housekeeper, it all works very well for them. She and Stewart are very happy together."

"I never hear of such a thing. Here, only spinsters work, men don't like wives to work."

"Well, it's time we changed that, do ye not think so? I have nae qualms about my wife doing whatever she wants to do." He couldn't bear being this close to her and not holding her. He made a desperate beckoning motion with his hands, and hesitantly, she got to her feet and moved, step by agonizing slow step, toward him. When she was close enough, he took her hands gently in his and tugged her closer still. She was trembling, her gaze uncertain.

He released her hands long enough to sign, "Please, lass, will ye no kiss me?"

She hesitated, and then bent down slightly, her nose awkwardly bumping his. Before she could pull away, he brought a hand up and slid it into her hair, fingers splayed, guiding her head so his lips met hers at just the perfect angle.

She tasted intoxicating, and it was all he could do to restrain himself, to keep from dragging her fully into his arms and pressing her body against his. Instead, he kept this first kiss gentle and teasing, brushing her mouth with his own, light as butterflies' wings. After a moment, she relaxed a little and opened her lips so he could more fully explore.

He deepened the kiss, and she shuddered and drew in a shaky breath, grateful for the generous folds of his kilt and the fact that he was sitting down.

But then she moved closer still, her body between his bent legs, and he couldn't bear not being able to hold her. He stood, using her shoulders to balance at first, standing on one leg and then bracing his good leg against the bed behind him so he could truly take her in his arms.

"Lovely Betsy, I'm that in love with ye, dearest lassie." He knew she couldn't hear his whispered endearment, but he wrapped his arms around her and drew her fully against him, reveling in her warmth, in her scent: lavender and sunshine and a hint of lemon to her silky hair. His hands stroked down her back, learning the delicate shape of her, wishing women didn't wear bloody corsets. He kissed her ear and her neck, learning the taste of her.

He drew back and smiled down at her before cupping her head and kissing her lips again. This time the kiss took fire, and they were both gasping when they drew apart.

She looked up at him, and her startling blue eyes were

wide and hazy with passion, her full lips swollen and rosy from his kisses. He knew she'd felt the evidence of his desire surging against her body, but she hadn't pulled away. Instead, she'd pressed her body against him.

"I love ye, Betsy." He knew she could lip read his low, husky declaration, and she gave a tremulous smile and nodded before she moved back a little. He took her hands in his and kissed each palm before he let her go, and then he lost his balance and tumbled back on the bed, wrenching his bad leg.

He grimaced and swore, and she giggled, putting a hand over her mouth. "I know that word, same word Noah says when cow kicks milk bucket over." Her cheeks and neck were flushed. She put up a hand to straighten her hair, managing only to loosen even more curls. They framed her oval face, and he thought he'd never seen any woman as beautiful.

"Very bad word," she teased, her eyes sparkling. "Annie says not to spell it even."

"Annie's right, and I humbly beg yer pardon," he signed. "I'll do my best to not swear again in yer company, but I can't promise. See, I'm no very good at this being crippled business. I'm a bad-tempered swine, so ye see what ye're maybe getting yourself into."

"Not crippled for long; leg will be better soon."

"Aye, I hope so." He wanted her to know what he feared. "But it's possible I'll always walk wi' a limp, Betsy."

She shrugged as if it wasn't an issue. "That will bother you?"

"Well, if I had me choice, I'd rather not have a gimpy leg," he smiled. "But I can ride fine, and I'm grateful to have a leg at all. The Indians knew how to curb infection. I want to learn what it was they used on me."

She tipped her head to the side. "You will go back to being Mountie?"

He shook his head. "No. I'll buy land, raise cattle. My five years is up this month, I'll be free then to do as I please as soon as I hand in my resignation." The words tumbled out, filled with excitement. "I'll claim a homestead, we'll marry when ye're ready, lass, I'll build ye a bonny house, we'll raise a family. I'll be a farmer." Joy filled him, because he knew now she had feelings for him, and he guessed that she'd agree to be his wife.

She nodded, but he could see the troubled expression on her face.

"What is it, sweet?"

"You want farm, I want to live in town," she said. "Can't have photography business out in the country, no one comes."

He realized at once the mistake he'd made. He tried to find a way around it, but before he could figure out how, Rose tapped on the half open door and after a discreet moment she stuck her head in, trying not to look shocked when she saw what James was wearing.

"Dinner's ready, Auntie says to come right away before the Yorkshire puddings fall."

Betsy nodded and made a washing motion with her hands and hurried out.

James put his crutch under his arm and hobbled into the dining room, wondering how he could have been such a flaming idiot. In one breath, he'd promised Betsy she'd have her business, and in the next he'd selfishly made plans that couldn't accommodate a photography studio. Had the wound on his head totally addled his brains? And just how the hell would he solve the problem? The solution was simple, he knew that. All he had to do was go back to practicing medicine.

And he also knew it was the one thing he could not do. Not now, not yet. Maybe never. His appetite, ravenous until now, fled entirely and he had to force himself to eat the sumptuous dinner Harriet had prepared in his honor.

Betsy studied her flushed face in the mirror above the bathroom washbasin, putting two fingers over her swollen lips. Who knew kisses could make her feel this way, make her lose all control? They never had before. She'd wanted him to do so much more than kiss her. And she'd never dreamed a man would look so masculine and irresistible in a skirt. Kilt, she corrected. She knew it was called a kilt, Aunt Harriet had a daguerreotype of her husband wearing one.

Her breasts throbbed against her chemise, the nipples tingling, sensitive, and her lower abdomen felt hot and full and achy. The intensity of her desire for James shocked her. So, this was what Annie had with Noah. Passion, friendship, total belonging. A desire for the beloved's body so powerful it overcame all reason. Certainly it made her stubborn insistence on only marrying a deaf man seem ridiculous. What was between her and James was far more encompassing than deafness or hearing.

She looked into her eyes in the mirror, biting her lip. It would be so easy to marry James. She thrilled at the thought of being his wife, of lying with him every night, loving together. She knew well the life of a farm wife and mother; she'd grown up learning from Annie what it required. She'd be good at it, and it was terribly tempting.

But if she abandoned her heart's desire, her yearning for her own photography business, Betsy knew she'd come to regret it, maybe not right away, but eventually. She hated to think of having to choose between James and photography. Either choice would leave part of her barren and heartbroken.

She leaned over the basin and splashed cold water over her hot cheeks. There had to be a way to have both of the things she wanted so much. There simply had to be.

Chapter Nine

When dinner was over, James asked Betsy if he could speak to her for a moment in private.

As Mrs. Coleman and Rose busied themselves carrying dishes to the kitchen, James led the way into the parlor.

Betsy watched him expectantly.

"I'm so very sorry for no realizing that my own plan was nae right for you," he began. "I'm not certain exactly what we'll work out, but please give me a chance to think of something. I promise ye, I'll find a suitable compromise. I want ye to have your photography studio, ye shall have it. I'll see to it."

She nodded. "I will think, too. Between us we can figure it out."

He was about to take a huge chance, but he couldn't wait any longer. He struggled to his feet and used the crutch to stand before her.

"I love ye with all me heart and soul, Betsy. I'd kneel if I could, but I can't. Will ye marry me, sweetheart?" He held his breath, heart hammering, waiting for her reply.

She looked at him for a long moment, and then she gave a shuddering sigh, nodded her head, and made the fisted up and down sign for yes.

"Betsy, ah, me darling lassie, ye've made me so happy." He took her in his arms and kissed her again and again, as a wave of relief rolled over him. "We'll go now and tell Miss Harriet and Rose. I wish I had champagne to celebrate. I'll get some right away."

But she shook her head. "Noah and Annie have to know first, before anyone. Noah was here for supplies two weeks ago, won't come again for a month. He says Annie is feeling well, just very tired, she is big with baby. I worry about her. I have two days off soon, we will go tell them then. Also, we must come to agreement on where we will live. For now, not tell anyone."

He was sorely disappointed. He wanted to announce their engagement in the Medicine Hat News, he wanted to call Harriet and Rose in and tell them. He wanted to announce it to all the men at the detachment; he wanted the entire world to know. But he also understood her desire to ride out to the Ferguson farm and tell Noah and Annie and the young ones first, even though it was frustrating not to be able to share his joy right this moment. Betsy's family came first. He felt a pang of regret for his own lost relatives.

At least now, though, he knew Betsy was as eager as he to come to an understanding that suited them both, to marry him sooner rather than later. Just knowing that and having her agree to marriage eased the anxiety that had gnawed at him all during the meal. He blew out a breath of relief and exuberance, wishing he could race outside and give a war whoop of triumph. Betsy was going to be his wife.

But nagging at him also was the knowledge that he hadn't yet been entirely honest with her. She knew nothing of his training as a surgeon. He hadn't told her he'd been trained as a doctor. Taking up his profession was the perfect solution to where they'd live, he knew that. There was a shortage of medical doctors everywhere on the prairies. There was plenty of opportunity for a trained surgeon here in Medicine Hat. Was it simple cowardice that kept him from going back to doing what he'd loved, what he'd trained for?

It was a question he'd asked himself many times, in the dead of night when he couldn't sleep. The answer wasn't a matter of physical cowardice, of that he was certain. In his time with the North-West Mounted, he'd fought hand-to-hand skirmishes, tracked murderers down and brought them to justice. He'd been afraid, but it hadn't stopped him doing his job. He didn't believe he was a coward, physically or emotionally.

No, it hinged on something else, something less clear-cut than simply being afraid of making mistakes like the one he'd made with Marguerite. It had to do with a part of him that had lost faith in himself, in his ability to make snap decisions in a medical emergency.

"As ye wish, me wee darlin'," he said to her now. "We'll go out to the farm, first opportunity." He stroked a hand down the side of her satin-soft cheek. "And we'll set our minds to where we'll settle. Two heads are better than one."

She smiled at him and shyly kissed his cheek. "Two hands also. Have to go, my turn to help with dishes."

"I'll help as well, but just not at this wee moment. As soon as I can stay on me feet longer than five minutes."

She gave him a knowing look. "Maybe you should write that promise and sign. Men I know not so good at doing dishes."

"You'll see, I'm very good at dishes. Cooking, too. The Mounted train their men in all the domestic chores."

"I believe when I see," she said, rolling her eyes. "You can prove to me after we marry," she said, blushing and blowing him a shy kiss.

He hobbled over to his bed and collapsed with a grin on his face.

For the next week, James alternately rested and exercised and silently exulted in his love for Betsy. The luxury of a soft bed, delicious meals, and lots of sleep meant that soon the acute pain in his leg dimmed to a dull ache.

He removed the bandage from his head, and spent hours each day stumping up and down the sidewalk outside the house, and inside climbing up and down the stairs. His leg was growing steadily stronger. He began to believe that eventually he'd even walk without a limp.

That hope, combined with the delight of seeing Betsy at the breakfast table before she rushed off to work, and spending time with her each evening, contributed to a deep sense of well-being and joy.

By unspoken mutual agreement, they didn't talk about the problem of living on a farm or in the city. Instead, they discussed books they loved, what their childhoods had been like. They argued over which writers were best. He liked Melville's Moby Dick and Cooper's The Last of the Mohicans. Betsy loved Dickens, which they agreed on, and Alcott's Little Women, which James hadn't read and didn't want to.

"Misogynist," she accused. "Not read because Miss Alcott is woman."

"Not at all," James insisted. "I enjoyed Bronte's Jane Eyre very much."

"Me also," she said fervently. "Love, love Jane Eyre."

"And I love you," he replied, gathering her into his arms.

They stole passionate kisses, always mindful of Harriet nearby.

James was keenly aware that Betsy slept in a room

directly over the parlor, just a staircase away. It was torture to have her so close, and many restless nights he imagined stealing up the stairs and into her bed. He knew from her fervent response when they embraced that she'd welcome him, but respect for Harriet forbade any such temptation. There was also the fact that he couldn't sneak anywhere—climbing stairs was still a laborious, noisy endeavor. The torture of wanting her desperately and being unable to make proper love to her reinforced his desire to marry her sooner rather than later.

One evening, Betsy brought down the framed photographs she'd taken of him. Usually confident, she was suddenly nervous as he studied them. She held her breath as James took his time studying the array.

"Yer a gifted photographer, lass. Considerin' what ye had to work with, these are nothing short of genius."

She blew out a relieved breath and pretended to wipe anxious perspiration from her forehead. Then she showed him the albums she'd put together of the random photos she'd taken while he was gone.

"This one," he said, studying one particular shot of a park bench under a tree by the river just at dusk. A man was sitting there, and she'd photographed him from the back, with the sun behind her, so just his outline showed, and she'd also caught her own shadow on the ground. There was something lonely and poignant about the photo, and when she'd developed it she realized it portrayed her own sense of isolation.

"I very much like this one," James said. "It reminds me of times when I've felt very alone. Yer an artist, Betsy. Ye really should have a public showing of these."

She felt herself flush with pleasure, but she also was thrilled that James experienced the same emotion she herself felt when looking at that portrait. It emphasized for her how compatible they were.

Except for the one area where they weren't compatible at all. The question of where they'd live was still unresolved.

The second week at Mrs. Coleman's, James rented a horse and buggy from the livery and rode out to the detachment. He gave his letter of resignation to Staff Sergeant Osler, said goodbye to the troops, and retrieved his belongings from his footlocker. He went to the barn and said a sad farewell to his horse, which belonged to the detachment.

"Ye've been a good, loyal friend, Ajax." He fed the horse an apple and stroked his nose. "Sorry to leave ye, old comrade."

It was the end of an era in his life, and he'd miss the men as well as the horse, but he felt no real regrets. He'd enjoyed the time he'd spent in the North-West Mounted. It had been an adventure, a young, single man's adventure. He had no desire to become a career policeman. What he wanted with all his heart was a more settled way of life, the life of a husband and, hopefully, a father.

A life as a rancher and farmer? All the way back to town, he was aware of the Gladstone bag with his medical equipment in it. He knew all too well that returning to practicing medicine was the ideal solution to Betsy's desire to have a photography studio in Medicine Hat. He was feeling more and more guilty at not telling her he was a physician. But returning to his profession was a decision he had to make himself, and each time he contemplated it, the image of his failed efforts to save his beloved sister and his wee nephew rose to haunt him.

Knowledge was essential as a doctor, but perhaps even more important was confidence, the ability to face any situation, no matter how dire, and without hesitation do the very best he knew to rectify the problem. He wasn't at all sure he could do so. He wasn't sure he ever would be able to.

"We will go to the farm tomorrow?" Betsy's fingers flew. She'd just come in from work, and the late October day was cold. Her cheeks were pink and her eyes sparkled as she flung off her warm shawl and coat. "Miss Evangeline says I can have next two days off."

James, screwdriver in hand, was repairing one of the dining room chairs. The back had come loose, and he was tightening screws. He was nearly fully recovered, and feeling increasingly bored and restless, so he'd taken to repairing whatever Hannah said needed fixing.

He glanced out the window and nodded. The weather was cold, but there was no sign of snow as yet. "Doesn't look like any storms are building, we should be fine."

Betsy clapped her hands and swung around in delight. "Can't wait to see Annie and everyone, tell them our news. We can leave early, livery will have horse for you."

"I'm thinking of buying one of me own." James laid down the screwdriver and caught her in his arms and kissed her thoroughly. "I'll ask Noah if he knows of a likely animal for sale." Hannah was out at a meeting of the church guild, and Rose hadn't come home yet. Betsy's cheeks were cold, but her mouth was warm and responsive.

"Sit down here wi' me for a wee while," he said. "There's something I'm needing to tell you." He'd been trying to find a private quiet moment all week, but there hadn't been an opportunity, and the longer he went without telling her, the more apprehensive he became.

"I will make tea first, still cold from walking home." She headed off to the kitchen and James was mentally rehearsing how best to explain himself to her when a loud knocking on the door sent him hurrying to answer.

James opened it, and Black Eagle said, "You must come now, baby is stuck, my daughter is dying. Come now, James Macleod, we must hurry. I have horses."

Chapter Ten

Ten minutes later, Betsy closed the door behind the two men and went back into the kitchen, her legs unsteady, her breath coming in short gasps.

She felt as if she'd fallen and had the breath knocked out of her. The tea tray, with biscuits and two china cups, sat on the table. She ignored it, collapsing in a chair and mentally going over and over in her mind the hurried words James had signed to her before he left with the Indian.

From the kitchen, Betsy had felt the cold blast of air from the door and gone down the hallway to see who was there. James and a tall Indian man in buckskin and a buffalo coat were having a heated discussion, and at first she couldn't understand much of what either was saying. They were arguing, James was shaking his head no, no, and the Indian man was saying something urgent about a baby, about a doctor.

Confused, she'd put a hand on James's arm and signed, "What? What is wrong?"

James's face was grim as he introduced Black Eagle. She remembered him telling her and Rose that he held the other man in high regard, that Black Eagle had saved his life.

The handsome Indian nodded solemnly when James introduced her. He silently watched the signs James made to her, not interrupting, but there was a sense of urgency about him, his body tense, his face grim.

"What he wants?" she asked James.

James hesitated. "His daughter is unable to deliver her baby. He wants me to come and tend to her."

Betsy shook her head in confusion. "But you are not doctor."

James met her puzzled gaze and shook his head. "I am a doctor, lass. I was nae honest wi' ye. I trained as a surgeon. That's what I was about to tell ye, before."

Shock went through her like a bolt of lightning. She shook her head, and her fingers felt frozen. She stumbled over the finger spelled words. "Doctor? But you never tell me this. You lie to me."

He shook his head and she could sense his guilt and his frustration. "I never actually lied, Betsy. I just never told ye the whole truth. I should have told ye long ago, lass. I'm that sorry."

Her hands were shaking so much that making signs was difficult. "Me, too, sorry." She looked at him, wondering how much else he'd lied about. She wondered whether she'd really known him at all. Did all men lie? She felt a huge chasm open in her heart. Hadn't he promised her total honesty? And all the while he'd been keeping this huge secret from her.

He rubbed a hand down his face and shook his head. "There's nae time to explain it all now, lass. I have tae go wi' him, I owe the man me life. I'll tell ye all about it when I get back. Please, darlin', give me a chance to explain?"

He waited, his troubled gaze intent on her face.

But she couldn't give him that reassurance. She stared at him as if he was a stranger.

He turned on his heel and retrieved a black Gladstone bag from the armoire where he kept his clothing. He reached out to draw her into his arms, but she stepped back, out of reach, holding her hands palms out. Don't touch me. She turned her back until she felt the cold air from the door opening and closing again.

Then he was gone.

Betsy collapsed on the chair James had mended. She wasn't sure how long she sat there. Without consciously deciding, she got up and went upstairs, packed her saddlebags, put on her brother's trousers with a warm wool skirt over the top.

She put on her riding boots, and tied a thick woolen shawl over her coat, adding the bright red mittens Annie had made. She pulled on a matching woolen cap, and then she took the mitts off again and wrote a careful note to Aunt Harriet, saying she'd gone to the farm, that she was needed, that she wasn't certain when she'd be back, and to please ask Rose to inform Miss Evangeline that she was so sorry, but she'd miss work, for how long she couldn't say.

Then she headed for the livery stable. She felt cold and empty, as if something vital inside had deserted her.

She needed to go home.

There was a huge harvest moon, and it seemed to light her way across the dark prairie. Surefooted Jingles knew the route, and Betsy let her choose her own pace.

Her chest felt tight, as though she couldn't draw breath, and her stomach was sick. In her mind, she went over and over the words James had said, the incredible words, that he was a doctor, a surgeon. Why hadn't he told her? She thought back over the discussion they'd had about where they'd live, about what he'd do now he was no longer a policeman. As a doctor, he could make a fine living in Medicine Hat, he must have realized that. So why hadn't he said something?

Her mind went round and round, always coming back to the fact that he'd lied, not a small white lie, but a huge fact about himself that changed many things. Always, like a loop, her mind kept asking why he would do such a thing.

As betrayed and angry as she felt, she still couldn't bring herself to believe that he didn't care about her, didn't love her. She went over and over the conversations they'd had, the kisses they'd shared. She didn't believe it was possible for a man to pretend that depth of emotion, but what did she really know about men?

There were good ones like Noah, and bad ones like George Watson. She'd believed that James was one of the good ones. Now, she didn't know what to believe. She only knew her heart ached as if it was breaking in half.

It was long past midnight when she rode into the farmyard. Jake came rushing toward the horse, barking and baring his teeth, but he quickly realized who it was and looked embarrassed, nearly wagging himself in half in apology and welcome.

She headed for the barn, hoping that no one had been disturbed by the dog, but she saw a candle's flickering light in the bedroom where Annie and Noah slept, and then a lantern being lit in the kitchen.

She was taking the saddle and bridle off Jingles by the time Noah appeared. He looked both surprised and disapproving, but he gave her a hug and then said, "You rode out by yourself? At night? Why would you do such a mad thing?" And then, looking at her more closely, he added in sign, "What's wrong, Bets?"

She started to sob, and couldn't stop.

Noah got the faintly desperate look he always wore

when his women cried. He patted her back and handed her a crumbled handkerchief from his coat pocket, then pointed toward the house.

"Go on inside, Annie's up. I'll take care of Jingles and bring your things."

Annie, in a blue flannel wrapper over her white nightdress, was adding wood to the heater when Betsy came in. She took one look at her sister's tearstained face and wrapped her arms around her, then led her to a chair close beside the stove.

In spite of her own misery, Betsy noticed how big Annie had gotten since she'd last seen her. She had felt the child in Annie's belly kicking even through her coat when Annie hugged her.

Annie helped take off Betsy's shawl and coat, and then waited while Betsy tugged off her boots. Her feet felt frozen, and she wriggled her toes and held them out to the warmth.

Annie pulled up a chair and sat beside her, touching Betsy's face with her fingers, coaxing Betsy to look at her.

"What's happened? What's wrong, sweet? Why are you crying? Are you hurt? Did someone hurt you?" Betsy's face reflected her concern and her love.

Hardly knowing where to begin, Betsy struggled with signing out the story of falling in love with James, of promising to marry him. She explained how she'd said she wanted the photography studio, and how he'd promised it would somehow come about.

"But he never told me he was doctor, never told me the truth. I only find out by accident." She described how the Indian had come to the door, and James had left with him.

"Lie to me, he lie to me." Betsy began to cry again. "Why? Why lie to me?"

Annie was obviously struggling to understand. She shook her head in puzzlement. "So he's a doctor—"

"Surgeon," Betsy interrupted. "Trained surgeon, lied to me, said he wanted to be farmer. Told me he loved me, wanted to marry." A fresh batch of tears came pouring down her cheeks, and Annie got up and brought a clean dishtowel, mopping at Betsy's face.

She sat down again and frowned. "So he's a doctor, Bets. Did he lie about loving you, too? Did he say now he doesn't want to marry?"

Betsy shook her head. "Went off with the Indian man, said no time to explain." Anger took over and dried her tears. "Had weeks to explain if he wanted. He is liar, same as George Watson."

Annie's eyes narrowed. "What really happened with Watson, Betsy? You never exactly told me, I think you should now."

Fingers trembling, unable to meet her sister's gaze, Betsy relayed the entire sordid story. By the time she'd finished, Annie was flushed and furious.

"He tried to rape you. You should have told Noah, he'd have threshed that scoundrel to within an inch of his life."

Betsy nodded. "I know, that's why I didn't say. Noah takes care of everyone, makes too much trouble for him to fight with snake like Watson."

Annie looked as if she might argue, but after a moment she nodded reluctant agreement. "Who knows what mischief a man like that might cause? And Noah is not so young as he once was."

They sat in silence for a long moment, their understanding mutual. Annie reached out and stroked Betsy's cheek.

"And Sergeant Macleod? Did he take advantage of you, Bets?"

Memories of the kisses they'd shared were vivid in her mind. She knew her cheeks blazed as she shook her head. "Not take advantage, no. Kissed me, nothing more," she confessed, not able to meet Annie's eyes as she added shyly, "I want more, James says wait. Wait until married."

Fresh tears filled her eyes. Now she'd never know what it felt like to lie with him.

"So all you're really upset about is this doctor thing, him not telling you he was a doctor?"

"All?" Betsy was furious all over again. "Lied to me. Easy to lie to deaf, we only know what we see, what is told to us. If he lies about this, what else is he not telling me?

How I can ever trust him again?"

Annie shook her head and began to answer, but Noah came in just then.

"So what's this all about?" he asked, coming over and holding out his big, work-worn hands to the heat rising from the stove. "What's got you so upset, Bets?"

The women met one another's eyes and unspoken agreement flashed silently between them.

"Womanly matters. Betsy's overwrought and needs to go to bed," Annie said. "And I'm tired as well, morning will be here far too soon." She laid a hand on her bulging belly, and immediately Noah lost interest in Betsy in concern for his wife. He reached down and helped her up.

"You need to rest, sweetheart, off to bed with you, I'll be in directly." He turned to Betsy. "Your saddlebags are just there by the door, you get off to your bed now. You can tell me what's amiss in the morning if you choose, we'll all be better off for a good night's sleep." He bent to the stove, using the iron poker to push the burning logs down before he loaded more in.

"Goodnight, Noah. Thank you." Betsy pressed a kiss on his cheek, retrieved her bulging saddlebags and headed off to her bedroom. She splashed some of the icy water from the pitcher into the basin, washed her hands and her face, which felt stiff from tears. She removed her layers of clothing and slid into a clean, sweet smelling flannel gown from the drawer, knowing as she laid down that she wouldn't sleep.

Her breath caught in a trembling sigh as she pulled the familiar quilts up over herself and closed her tired eyes for a moment.

The next thing she was aware of was the gray dawn light trickling in the window. She'd been dreaming of Zachary. They were walking in a field, and he was holding her hand and telling her something important. She could always hear in her dreams, and even now, still muzzy with sleep, she imagined his deep, soothing voice inside her head. He was telling her how happy he was, and that she should be happy too. He wanted that for her. He loved her, Zachary said.

She thought of James, and hurt and the deep sense of betrayal pierced her heart. She threw the blankets back, shivering in the early morning chill. Quickly, she washed in the icy water from the pitcher, hurrying into her clothes.

In the kitchen, Noah was making coffee, tipping the grounds from the coffee mill into the old enamel pot, adding water. He was the only one up, and he smiled at her, and when the coffeepot was set on the hot part of the cook-stove to perk, he asked if she wanted to come help with the chores.

The barn was warm with animal heat, and they set to work, milking, pitching hay into the manger for the four cows, shoveling manure from the stalls, dumping the kitchen bucket of slops into the trough for the pigs, measuring grain for the horses and cows. The familiar routine was comforting to Betsy. She and Noah had often worked side by side like this, using a few old abbreviated signs to indicate what needed done, or comment on the animals.

When they were done, he took a seat on a bale of hay and pointed to another. Betsy sat facing him.

"You want to tell me what had you so upset last night?"

Betsy thought about it, and then nodded. With lightning fast signs, she told Noah the whole story of James's courtship, of their plans to marry, and his deceit about being a doctor. She left out only the part about George Watson.

"James lie to me," she concluded. "Why he didn't ever tell me the truth, that he was doctor? We talked about what he would do after he left the police, he only said he would farm, but I want studio, in Medicine Hat. It would have been easy for him to be doctor there. Now I think maybe he doesn't really want marriage."

But even as she signed it, she knew that wasn't true. Through the whole of their time together, it was James who steadfastly told her of his feelings, his love for her. But there was still lingering doubt about one thing. "Maybe because I am deaf he doesn't think he has to tell me truth. Easy to fool deaf woman." Her bitterness tasted like bile in her throat.

Noah hadn't said anything all during her outburst. He sat, deep in thought, for what seemed a long time.

"I only met Macleod the once. I liked the man and trusted him, or I'd never have allowed him to accompany you back to the Hat. But men can be deceitful; you're right about that. What do you think he wants from you, Bets?"

She thought about it and then shrugged. "I have nothing except myself," she signed. "He says he wants to marry with me, have a family, be happy."

"And what do you want, Bets?"

She knew, deep down. "Same." It was true. But there was more. "I want my own business, photography business. I need this, to prove it is something I can do. Always, there has been much I can't do because I am deaf. I need this to prove to me that I am smart, capable person."

"And what does James say about you having your own business after you marry?"

"He wants this for me also." There was no question in her mind about that. He'd told her about his cousin, a woman doctor, how well that marriage worked. "But he doesn't tell the truth about what would make it possible, for him to work as doctor in Medicine Hat. He never tell me that. So maybe not want me to have it so much, yes?"

Noah shrugged. "I don't know the man well enough to say. But keeping secrets isn't uncommon. You remember that Annie and I had told each other big fat lies before we were married."

Betsy nodded and smiled. She remembered well, because some of those lies were about her, about the fact that she wasn't Annie's daughter, and that she was deaf.

"I know how you're feeling, Bets, because I was furious that morning when I met the train and saw you both. I felt betrayed when you and Annie arrived. I wanted to pack you both back to where you'd come from. The only reason I didn't, there wasn't a train going east that day. I needed help, both on the farm and with my father. I wanted an older woman, a woman who could cook and work on the farm with me."

Betsy swallowed hard. She'd never really appreciated how tenuous that new beginning had been for her and Annie.

"But people don't always come in the form you want them to. You were sick, coughing like you had the consumption, and you both were pitifully skinny, looked like a strong wind would blow you away. I needed a wife who was strong, who could work hard. I believed Annie was much older than she actually was. She told me in her letters that you were her daughter."

"Why you didn't send us back?"

He smiled at her, that warm, loving smile that had always made her feel safe.

"Because you were deaf. See, Annie thought that would be the one thing that would decide me for certain to send you both away. Instead, it was what convinced me you had to stay."

Betsy shook her head, puzzled. "I don't understand."

"Neither did I, not for a long time. At first I thought, what kind of man would send a child away for something that wasn't her fault? And then I saw that you were like an angel sent to make my father's last months easier and happier. You being deaf was the biggest gift to him, and to me."

She looked at him in wonder. Noah had never said much about her being deaf, just questions at first to Annie about certain signs, about how to best communicate with her. He learned her signs quickly and always talked directly to her, never using Annie to interpret.

She'd never considered her deafness a gift; that was certain. Often, it had been a major hindrance, preventing her from going to school, isolating her from other people, always making her different.

"Sometimes we're so scared of something bad happening, we find a way to make it happen, just to get it over with," Noah went on. "I've done it a couple times, at least until I figured out what I was doing. I tried to drive Annie away by being a bad-tempered ass after I fell in love with her, because I was bone-deep scared of her leaving me. Better get it over with, I thought."

Bets thought about that. Slowly, she figured out what Noah was trying to tell her.

"You think I am scared James will change his mind when he finds out what it is like to live with deaf woman?"

"Yes." Noah's fist went up and down emphatically in the sign for yes. "I think deep down you're scared of losing him, the way I was with Annie. Him not telling you he was a doctor, I think there was probably a good reason for that, maybe something he has trouble talking about. Men aren't good talkers, Bets."

She was trying to absorb what he'd said, trying to be honest enough to find out if it was true.

"There's a saying. Don't throw the baby out with the bathwater." He smiled at her and stood up, picking up the two pails of fresh milk.

She took the basket of eggs, trying to decipher the saying in relation to herself. Together, they headed for the house.

The cabin was small and swelteringly hot from the press of bodies. James was relieved that there was a cabin at all—he'd expected a teepee. A woman was screaming in agony when Black Eagle opened the door. The women gathered in the small kitchen stood back silently, their dark eyes filled with helpless pity, as Black Eagle led James into an even smaller bedroom.

Two elderly Indian women were bending over the bed, and when they moved away, in the dim light from a single lamp James saw Black Eagle's daughter.

She was hardly more than a child. Her long midnight black hair was sweat-soaked, her dark-skinned, handsome face twisted in agony. Her arms were thin, the bulge of her belly huge. She wore only a blue cotton smock, and blood stained the sheets beneath her. The women had propped her up on pillows. The smell in the room was pungent and thick, a combination of urine, feces, blood and herbs—and fear.

"My daughter, Raven." Black Eagle said something to her, and her eyes, red and sunken and staring, flicked toward James. An instant later, her features convulsed and the screaming began as her body twisted and writhed as a contraction seized her, her body trying in vain to expel the child trapped within her. At the height of the contraction, her eyes rolled back in her head and she fell into a faint.

James moved quickly, checking her pulse, lowering her head, using a cool cloth on her wrists and forehead as he tried to still the trembling of his hands. He felt he was in the midst of his own worst nightmare.

The journey here had been fast and desperate, Black Eagle galloping ahead, James following on the swift little Indian pony Black Eagle had brought for him. There'd been no opportunity for conversation, and with each mile, James had envisioned the stunned, accusing look on Betsy's face, the way she'd turned away from him.

He could only pray that she'd forgive him. He could

no longer imagine his life without her. Why had he been such an idiot, not telling her the whole truth about himself? And what exactly was he going to do at the scene which awaited him?

The longer he rode the more apprehensive he became. If Black Eagle was right, if his daughter couldn't deliver her child vaginally, James would be faced with operating—caesarian section, the very same operation that had killed his sister. The operation he'd sworn to himself he would never again attempt. The only other solution when a woman couldn't deliver was to remove the embryo in pieces, cut the wee living thing up with a scalpel inside the mother. It was a scene from hell, and his belly roiled at the very thought.

Now, however, seeing this poor girl-woman in agony, something instinctual in him took over. In his heart, in his deepest being, he was still a doctor. His vow as a surgeon was to ease suffering, to save lives if at all possible. This poor young woman would surely die if nothing was done.

He set down his bag, and the dread and inner trembling abated. Here was his patient, and there was a job to be done.

"I need hot, boiled water, quickly, and clean rags."

A basin was brought, and he rolled his shirtsleeves high and scrubbed his hands and arms with soap from his bag. He asked for, and was given, a second basin, in which he immersed the instruments from his bag in a strong solution of carbolic acid, as Sir Joseph Lister had taught to prevent antisepsis.

He spoke to the girl softly, not certain she could even hear or understand. "Raven, I'm going to examine you, we'll figure out together how best to help you and your baby." He had no idea whether she understood him or not. She'd come out of her faint, but it was obvious she was nearing the end of her strength.

Careful examination proved that the baby was lodged crosswise, high up in Raven's body. James made several desperate futile efforts at moving it, and then another contraction began. Raven was trembling, sweat pouring from her body, but her skin felt cold and clammy. Her screams were weak, her eyes glassy.

Was it already too late? If he did nothing, she would surely die. But if he operated—

James knew the decision he made in this moment would determine the rest of his life. Raven's as well. He could not bring himself to slice up a living child if there was any alternative.

"Scrub the kitchen table and spread a sheet over it," James ordered. "Clear everyone out except for one woman to assist me."

Chapter Eleven

Black Eagle, hovering in the doorway, gave swift, guttural orders. James slid his arms around the slight figure on the bed, carrying her to the table. The room was empty, but terrified faces were pressed against the single window, and the woman Black Eagle had chosen was standing beside the table.

"I'll need more light, more lanterns," he ordered, and the women nodded and hurried out, returning in moments with two more, which were swiftly lit as he laid out his surgical instruments. James gestured at the basin, indicating she should wash hands and arms, which she did.

"What's your name?" he asked her, but it was Black Eagle, standing guard by the door, who answered.

"Willow," he said. "My sister. She understands you, but speaking, not so much."

"Pleased to make your acquaintance," James said to her, and then carefully administered the chloroform to Raven, soaking a bit of cotton in the bottom of a small glass and holding it under Raven's nose. He kept his fingers on her pulse, and paid close attention to her breathing.

When he judged her to be deeply unconscious, he carefully washed her abdomen in carbolic and picked up the scalpel, aware that the child must be delivered quickly. The chloroform would soon have a dangerous effect on its breathing and heartbeat.

For an instant he stood frozen as Raven's face became Jenny's, and scarlet blood clouded his vision, blood spurting out that he couldn't stop, the slight weight of the dead blue child in his hands---

He drew in a deep breath and with extreme effort of will banished the horrible vision. He breathed a heartfelt prayer, and made a swift and confident transverse incision in the lower segment of the uterus. Blood oozed, and he blotted it away, showing Willow how to do it.

Willow made a sound somewhere between an exclamation and a prayer, but she did as he directed, after a moment seeming to anticipate what he needed.

The bag of waters broke under the scalpel's sharp edge, and James reached in and lifted out the baby, a large, well-formed boy with a thick mop of black hair glued to his scalp with birth fluids.

Swiftly, James clamped and cut the umbilical cord, tying it off with a piece of string he'd prepared. He swiped the boy's mouth, hung him upside down, patted the tiny back, and an outraged wail sounded in the room.

Murmurs of amazement passed between Willow and

Black Eagle as James handed the crying baby to Willow, and turned back to his other patient, once again checking Raven's pulse and breathing. The pulse was feathery, her breathing uneven, and he knew he needed to hurry.

Carefully, he removed the placenta. He'd threaded several surgical needles with silk, and now he began the painstaking, slow job of repairing the uterus. Sweat formed on his forehead, and he reached for a towel to wipe it off, but Willow anticipated his need.

It seemed to take hours of careful, small stitching, but at last it was done, and James began the task of suturing the abdominal skin, crouching over his patient, straining to see in the flickering light.

When the stitching was at last finished, James straightened his aching back and turned to Black Eagle. "Do you have any of the herbs the women used on me, that kept the wound from developing septicemia?"

Black Eagle, now cradling his swaddled grandson, spoke at length to Willow, and from a basket she drew out a handful of herbs. She began preparing them, pounding them into powder, mixing them with boiled water.

James was concerned that Raven was still deeply unconscious. Had he misjudged the quantity of chloroform? He'd been extremely careful, but she'd been weak before he administered it. Had it damaged her heart? He'd witnessed cases of death from anesthesia.

Willow now had the herb preparation ready, and James

applied it liberally to the stitched abdomen. He then used lengths of clean cloth to bind up Raven's abdomen, and Willow washed Raven and slipped a fresh chemise over the girl's head and down her bandaged body.

Willow then stripped the soiled sheets from the bed and replaced them with fresh, and James lifted Raven from the table and laid her back on the bed. He again checked her pulse and her breathing. They seemed stronger, but perhaps it was his own wishful thinking.

"She will wake up?" Black Eagle's voice was soft and anxious.

"Yes," James answered, pretending a confidence he was far from feeling. But no matter what happened now, it was out of his hands. He examined the baby more thoroughly, confirming that the wee boy was perfect in every way. He was well formed, broad shouldered, with long arms and legs. He opened coal dark eyes and gave James an accusing look, which made him smile.

"He's a braw wee mannie," James declared before handing him back to Black Eagle.

He then gratefully accepted a cup of strong tea and a piece of bannock when Willow offered it, and the three of them waited. The tense atmosphere was punctuated now and then by the baby's cries, but the adults were silent, watchful. James brought a stool and sat beside the bed, monitoring his patient.

It was about forty minutes later when Raven at last

moved restlessly and then opened her eyes. James didn't understand the words, but he knew what she was asking. She was calling for her baby. He felt a huge burden drop from him as Willow hurried in and settled the tightly bundled child in his mother's arms.

Black Eagle brought a young, handsome man in, introducing him as Panther, the baby's father. James shook his hand, congratulating him on his son.

Raven handed the baby over, and Panther's smile stretched from one ear to the other as he looked down into the crumpled little face. He said something to Raven, and although James didn't understand the words, their meaning was plain. It was a statement of wonder, of pride, of hope for the future. It sounded like love, and it made James so lonely he could barely breathe.

It was time to go. He gathered up his instruments, cleansed them, repacked his Gladstone bag, and took his leave of Willow and Black Eagle.

"I'll need to borrow a horse to get back to town," he said, but Black Eagle had already arranged it. He led James outside to where a beautiful coal-black stallion was pawing the ground, annoyed at the fine, hand tooled leather saddle on his back and the bit between his teeth.

Black Eagle said the stallion's name, but it was unpronounceable to James. He climbed on the animal's back, and the horse skittered and snorted. It took effort, but James brought him under control.

"Thanks, I'll get him back to ye tomorrow," James said, but Black Eagle shook his head.

"He is yours, Doctor James Macleod."

James thought of protesting. He knew that Black Eagle and his tribe had little of value except their horses, but he also knew it was bad manners to refuse a gift. Black Eagle had told him so on their long journey together.

"I thank ye, my friend." For far more than the horse and saddle. Black Eagle had trusted him with the lives of his daughter and grandson, even knowing how he'd failed before. He'd had faith where James had none. He'd been willing to gamble, to trust, and in the process had given James something back he'd thought he'd forever lost. It was a gift that James felt he could never repay.

Black Eagle nodded once, held up a hand in farewell, and headed back into the cabin. James found the trail and rode slowly back to Medicine Hat. He had no idea how late it was. The stars were bright overhead, and the moon was low in the western sky, so perhaps morning was not far off. It had been a night of terror and realization; a night of gut-wrenching fear, and hope, and finally, of triumph.

His operating skills were still there. He'd broken through his painful barriers of self-doubt and disgust. The memory of his sister and his lost little nephew would always be with him, but the paralyzing guilt had eased, making it possible to move ahead with his life as a healer. He'd made a terrible mistake, and as a doctor and a surgeon he'd likely make more, because he wasn't a miracle worker. He was human, with all the human frailties. He was ready to embrace his career again, pursue his calling with all of his energy and talent, and it was a huge relief to him. It was exciting.

The question that gnawed at him was, would the woman he loved be at his side?

Chapter Twelve

Betsy spent the day trying to make things easier for her sister. Annie was big with this baby, bigger than Betsy remembered her being with the girls. With the twins, of course, she'd been enormous, but Noah had said that old Doc Kinsade didn't seem to think she was carrying twins this time. She was obviously tired and worn out, however. The baby was expected to come in the next two weeks, and Noah was furious with the doctor.

Noah had arranged months ago that Kinsade was to call every couple of days at least, but there was an outbreak of influenza, and Doc hadn't been around in over a week. When Noah rode over to forcibly bring him to the farm, Doc's wife said Kinsade was in bed with the flu.

Noah was torn between dragging the old doctor home with him in spite of the illness and not wanting to bring the influenza home to his family.

So he'd stuck close to the house. He didn't want to leave Annie alone during the day, and he was mightily pleased to have Betsy there. After breakfast he took the twins and went off in the wagon to mend a fence that the antelope had knocked down, leaving clear instructions as to where he'd be should they need him.

Betsy, with Mary Elinora's help, stripped and re-made all the beds with fresh sheets, and then hauled and heated water, set up the hand-operated washing machine Noah had proudly ordered from Chicago, and spent most of the day washing clothes. It was chilly out, but sunny, and the fresh breeze meant the clothes would dry on the outside lines.

The little girls, Nellie and Alice, brought in wood and helped carry baskets of clean clothing from the line to the table for Annie to fold. Betsy let her, because it was work that could be done sitting down.

Doing the washing was hard, backbreaking work, and by the end of the afternoon Betsy was sweaty and tired. Annie made a pot of tea and a batch of oatcakes, and they sat around the table with a jar of rhubarb jam and a dish of butter, enjoying the break. A stew simmered on the stove, and a batch of yeast biscuits were rising for supper, whenever Noah and the boys made it back.

"Someone's coming," Alice announced, peering out the window. The little girls raced out the door. Visitors weren't a daily occurrence, and they were excited.

Annie went to the window and looked out. "It's your James," she signed.

Betsy's heart began to hammer. Washing and pegging

clothes had given her lots of time to think about her conversation that morning with Noah. He'd forced her to consider her feelings and reactions in a way she hadn't before. But she still wasn't sure he was right—was she using anger and her sense of betrayal to drive James away—because she was so afraid he'd leave her anyway? She hated to admit it, but it was also hard to deny it. Yes, he'd been less than honest with her. But perhaps she'd also been less than honest with herself.

She resisted the urge now to go to the mirror on the wall by the washbasin and fix her hair or sponge off her face. He could see her exactly as she was, hot, sweaty, disheveled.

A few moments later, James came in, accompanied by the three girls. Nellie was holding his hand. He stood just inside the door, and he spoke to Annie, but his worried eyes were on Betsy.

"Good day, Annie. I hope I find you well?" He swept his hat off, and Alice took it and his coat, hanging them on a peg on the coat rack. "Betsy?"

The look he gave her was a question too complicated to answer. She nodded her head in acknowledgment of his presence, but that was all.

"Come in, James, and yes, thank you, I'm fine." Annie gestured to the table. "We're just having tea and scones, please join us."

Annie brought a cup and a plate to the table, and the

girls found cutlery and a chair. Annie poured, handed James the cup and the plate of scones.

James was across from Betsy, and she avoided looking at his eyes.

"The girls and I were just about to feed the chickens, if you'll excuse us, James?" Annie struggled to her feet, and Betsy could see the little girls complaining that they'd already fed the chickens.

Betsy shot her sister a pleading look, but Annie was already herding her daughters briskly out the door.

Annie was deserting her. Betsy's heart was hammering against her ribs as if it was determined to break free, but she tried not to show how nervous she felt. She sat with her head down for what seemed a long time before James reached across and gently touched her arm to draw her attention.

"Please, Betsy. Please, sweetheart, we have to talk," he signed.

Something broke free in her, and she lashed out at him. "You should have told me you were doctor," she signed vehemently. "First day we met, I asked you. You should have told me then."

He sighed and nodded, and against her will, she saw how weary he was, how bloodshot his eyes were.

"You're right, lass. I should have told you. I'm so sorry I didn't. Will you let me try and explain?"

She didn't reply, but she waited and watched his

hands.

"I told you my sister died in childbirth, my wee nephew along with her."

Betsy nodded.

"The part I left out was that it was my doing." He went on rapidly, describing the argument with the other doctor, his own certainty that Marguerite had eclampsia, that caesarian section was the only chance to save her or her babe. He described McFee's anger and disdain for new ideas, his father and Brian's uncertainty.

"They finally agreed with me, and I began the operation. But Marguerite had a seizure while I was operating, and my scalpel slipped. I nicked an artery, and she bled to death in seconds."

Betsy made a sound in her throat, horrified and shocked by what his fingers were saying. He was sickly white beneath the tanned skin. His eyes remained steady on hers, but she could see the anguish in them. "The baby wasn't far enough along to save. His wee lungs were not developed enough. They both died, and it was my doing."

He heaved a sigh and went on, telling her of the terrible aftermath, the other doctor accusing him of malpractice, the investigation, the trial. Worst of all was the horror of feeling that his family blamed him for Marguerite's death, as much as he blamed himself.

"So I ran away, Betsy. I came here to Canada to forget. I told no one that I was a surgeon, until I met Black Eagle.

God knows why I told him, but I did."

"His daughter. Her baby. They are alive?"

For the first time, his grim features relaxed and he smiled. "Both alive and well, she has a bonny wee son."

"You did this same thing, this—" her fingers stumbled over the word and she shuddered at the very thought of opening a woman's belly to deliver a baby. "This--- Caesarian—this operation—you did it on her? On Black Eagle's daughter?"

He nodded. "I did. There was no other way. She would have died, and the babe with her."

"I am glad. But it was wrong of you not to tell me you are doctor, James. Hurt me very much. I feel you don't trust me. Now I think I can't trust you."

He half rose to his feet, as if to come and take her in his arms, but she waved him away, and he sank back into the chair with a sigh.

"It's no you I di'nae trust, lass. I'd trust ye with my life. Can ye no understand it's myself I didn't trust? I lost my confidence. I lost the certainty a surgeon has to have, the surety that whatever he attempts, he's doing his best for his patient."

"And now?" She'd noticed that he'd said he didn't trust himself before.

"I'll never forget Marguerite and the babe. I'll never forget I made that fatal mistake. But I think I can use those memories now to be a better doctor." He paused for a long moment, and she saw tears shimmer in his eyes. "But without ye as my wife, Betsy, my life will be empty. I promise ye I'll not give you cause to distrust me, ever again. I'll love and cherish ye all the days of my life. Will ye no forgive me, lassie?"

She looked at him, at the ravages the past days had created. He needed a shave. He needed a wash; there were dirt smears on his hands and down one cheek. He needed to sleep; his eyes were beyond bloodshot, and there were weary lines etched deep beside his eyes and mouth that hadn't been there before.

She remembered what Noah had asked her that morning. He'd said, *What do you want, Bets?*

She knew, but it was so hard to let her barriers down. It was so hard to trust. She'd have to learn to do it one day at a time, because she knew she wanted this man, this hearing man, as her lover, as her husband, as the father of her babies—as her support, her silent partner, in her photography business. In her life. All day she'd thought about something else Noah had said.

He'd accepted her and Annie into his home—into his heart—not in spite of her deafness, but because of it. It was the first time she'd seen her deafness as an asset instead of a liability. Maybe that was how James viewed it too—as a positive thing instead of a negative.

Slowly, she pointed a finger at her chest. Then she made a gentle fist with both hands, and she crossed them over her heart, as if she was hugging him close. Then she pointed at him.

I----- Love----- You.

It was all that needed said.

Her lips formed the words, but it was the sign that brought joy spreading across his weary features, that brought him to his feet. He made the evocative gesture back at her, and then he took her in his arms, and his lips came down on hers.

The kiss was both passionate and gentle, a silent promise made and received in the universal language of the heart, interrupted by a frantic Mary Elinora pulling at Betsy's arm.

"Come quick, Bets, come quick, Mama's pains have started, she's lying on the ground and she can't get up."

Chapter Thirteen

Christmas Eve

Noah stamped his feet on the rug just inside the kitchen door and tugged off his boots. It had been a mild December with very little snow, but that looked as if it was changing. It had gotten cold in the night, and now flakes were sifting down like feathers.

He breathed in deeply, taking in the smells of baking, of fresh bread, of apples and cinnamon and mincemeat. The wedding cake, three tiers high and covered in icing as white as the falling snow stood on the sideboard. A monstrous ham, dotted with cloves, sat ready for slicing, and the smell of roasting beef mingled with the fresh odor of pine coming from the decorated Christmas tree in the far corner of the room.

The pantry was filled to overflowing. His women had made certain there'd be no one going hungry today.

Mary Elinora, Alice, and little Nellie wore voluminous white aprons over their new green velvet dresses. They were washing, drying, and putting away the last of the pots and pans that had been used in the mammoth food preparation.

The girl's excitement showed in their sparkling eyes and in their sweet, high voices.

"Daddy, Daddy, hurry up, you have to wash and get ready quick, Mama says Reverend Boxdale will be here any minute," Mary Elinora ordered. "And so will the Hopkinses. Rose and her Auntie and the important policeman are all coming from Medicine Hat. Rose is going to do Auntie's hair, I can't wait to see what she does with it."

"Yes, Daddy, hurry!" the two smaller girls chimed in, and Noah grabbed them up, tucking one under each arm. They squealed and kicked in delight.

"Who told you squirts you could boss your father this way?" he teased, giving Mary Elinora a quick kiss on her flushed cheek.

"Mama did," the little girls giggled.

"Where is your mama?"

"Feeding Willie *again*. She's trying to fill him up good so maybe he'll last through the ceremony. Then she's going to help Auntie Bets get dressed, and we're going to help, too," Mary Elinora pronounced. "But only if we finish these dishes. Come on, you two, stop being giddy and get busy."

Noah set the girls down and then washed hurriedly in

the basin in the corner before he went into his and Annie's bedroom.

Annie smiled at him. She was sitting in the nursing rocker, and baby Willie was feeding at her breast, tiny fists flying, legs kicking, making the desperate snuffling gulps that signaled he once again believed he was on the verge of starvation.

Noah went over and kissed Annie, not a quick peck, a deep, intimate lengthy kiss that left them both flushed and a little breathless. He stroked a finger across the baby's downy cheek.

"How's our little glutton?"

From the moment he'd exploded into the world that memorable afternoon, William Edward Ferguson had made everyone aware that he was hungry. Broad shouldered and long, he'd weighed in at over ten pounds, the largest of Annie's babies and the most vocal.

He'd also been the most eager to be born—Annie's labor lasted less than twenty-five minutes. Noah had arrived home just in time to welcome his new son, and to be forever grateful that the doctor about to become his brother-in-law was there to deliver Willy and care for Annie.

"Where are the boys?" Annie said. "They'll need to wash up and get their good shirts and trousers on, I laid them out on their bed."

"I heated a washtub of water on the stove in the barn,

they were scrubbing up when I came in, so they should be close behind me. James is out there supervising. He'll wash and dress as soon as they're done."

"And he's made the room out there ready for him and Betsy?" The house would be filled to the brim with guests, and it was Noah who'd suggested to James that he and Betsy should spend their wedding night in the room in the barn. It was warm, and most of all, it was private.

"He has. Clean sheets and cases, fresh towels, and that quilt you made for them. A bottle of champagne, some fancy glasses."

Annie nodded, satisfied. "Is he nervous, Noah? Betsy's like water on a griddle, hopping from one thing to another, never finishing anything, completely out of sorts and cranky to boot."

Noah laughed. "Never saw a man as steady and sure of what he's doing as James."

"Lucky we were married before we ever laid eyes on one another," Annie said. "You'd have backed out right then and there."

"I guess God knew what was best for me, even if I didn't," Noah said.

"Do you think that's the way of it, that whatever's meant to be, happens in spite of us?"

Willie gave a huge sigh and released Annie's nipple with a pop. He went quiet and limp, a thin trickle of milk leaking from his mouth, eyes crossing and then shutting tight into contented slumber.

Annie lifted him and gently patted his back.

"I do believe that's the way of it," Noah said, doffing his work shirt and trousers, pulling on the fresh ones Annie had laid out for him. "Betsy swore up and down she'd never marry a hearing man, and now she is. James figured he'd never do any doctoring again, and he's right back in the thick of it. He says he's already got more patients than he can handle."

A huge belch erupted from their son, and Annie and Noah laughed together.

"So maybe the best thing to do is fuss over the small things and let the big ones take care of themselves," Noah pronounced.

It was the small things that were making Betsy half crazy.

One of the tiny buttons on the back of her wedding gown had popped off and gone skittering under the bed. When she went after it, her hair, freshly washed, wild and absurdly curly, caught on the bedspring. Betsy was waiting for the arrival of Rose, who'd promised to do something wonderful with the mess. It had taken the combined efforts of her three little nieces to release it without tugging out a chunk of her scalp.

She'd been unable to eat either breakfast or lunch, and little Alice, in a fit of giggles, told her that everyone could hear her stomach rumbling. The girls ran to get her a bun and some cheese, lest the stomach thing happen during the ceremony.

The ceremony. She was so nervous she wasn't sure she'd be able to lip read what the minister was saying. What if she said or did the wrong thing at the wrong time? Mary Elinora had promised to interpret his words, but what if her niece got it wrong?

She wanted photographs of her wedding, and she'd tried to teach Rose how to operate her large indoor camera, but Rose didn't have a knack for it. Noah had offered, and Betsy had done her best to teach him, too, but she didn't think he was any better at it that Rose.

And where *was* Rose? She was riding out from Medicine Hat with Staff Sergeant Osler and Aunt Harriet, but they hadn't arrived yet. The snow was coming down harder every minute. the minister wasn't here yet either. There were so many things that could go wrong.

Most of all, Betsy wanted—she needed-- to talk to James, but Annie insisted it was bad luck for them to see one another on their wedding day. That was just stupid, Betsy fumed. There were urgent things she needed to discuss with him. But the entire family had been vigilant about keeping them apart.

Just when she was certain her wedding day was going to be a colossal disaster, everything happened at once.

The carriage with the Medicine Hat guests drew into

the farmyard at the same time as Reverend Boxdale and his wife arrived in their sleigh, with the Hopkins family close behind them in a democrat.

Rose came flying upstairs, Annie and the little girls close behind her, and Betsy immediately felt better. Her sister and her best friend, not to mention her nieces, would see her through this ordeal.

Annie took charge, helping her into the white silk dress Miss Evangeline had made for her. She'd sold the bolt of heavy white oriental silk to Noah at a huge discount, but would take nothing for designing and sewing the dress. It was long sleeved and high-necked, with delicate lace across the shoulders and bodice and a wide satin ribbon as a belt. She'd cut the silk on the bias, so the deceptively simple design moved like water over Betsy's slender curves.

Annie, mindful of her guests, shooed the little girls out, leaving the two young women alone as Rose expertly gathered up Betsy's unruly auburn hair and deftly wove it into an intricate chignon, with a few alluring curls allowed to escape and frame her face.

"Have you had letter from Philip?" Betsy signed, staring into the cheval mirror as Rose worked on her hair.

Philip Amundson, Rose's beau for the better part of a year, had suddenly and inexplicably quit his job at his father's law office the month before, climbed on a train, and headed for Vancouver. All he'd said to Rose was that he was sorry, but he needed to see more of the world before he settled down.

Rose, who had a temper, had said a great deal to him. She'd also smacked him soundly across the face.

"No." Rose shook her head, and her eyes sparkled with anger. "Never want to see or hear from him again. He's a weasel. Don't nod your head like that, be still so I can get this secured."

Betsy felt terrible for her friend. Rose had insisted she and Betsy would have a double wedding as soon as Betsy came to her senses and accepted James's proposal. Rose had been totally certain of Philip's intentions. She'd confided to Betsy that she and Philip had had sex, and that she'd loved it, but when Philip left, Rose was sick with fear until her monthlies came and she knew she wasn't pregnant.

The one thing Betsy wasn't anxious about was her wedding night. She was looking forward to it. James had been the one who insisted they wait. "I want it to be perfect for ye, lass, not something we have to hurry or sneak about to enjoy. I want to hold ye in me arms the whole night long, as me wife."

For the last month, Betsy had taken great delight in teasing him, growing bolder with her kisses and caresses. He'd told her he'd make her pay for testing him almost beyond endurance. It was a punishment she couldn't wait to receive.

Rose stuck one last hairpin into her creation and then drew Betsy to her feet, surveying her critically before she nodded approval.

"You are a vision, Betsy Tompkins. James is going to just swoon when he sees you. Now, I can hear Reverend Boxdale playing the violin, he told me to listen for it, that it would mean everything's ready for you. So, Noah will be up in a minute to conduct us down." She checked her own green silk dress in the mirror, patted her golden hair into place, and pinched her cheeks. Then she wrapped her arms around Betsy and held her close. Her eyes were bright with tears as she drew away and signed, "You are my dearest, bestest friend in all the world. I am so happy for you. James is a fortunate man."

The living room was stuffy, filled with the myriad scents of too many people crowded together, of food, of pine from the Christmas tree, of wood burning in the stove.

James couldn't seem to draw in a deep breath. His gut was tight, and he had to keep clearing his throat. Staff Sergeant Osler stood beside James, resplendent in his immaculate red uniform. James had asked him to be his groomsman.

The haunting notes of the violin rose over the excited chatter of the family and guests, signaling that the minister was ready. The man was an accomplished violinist, and the music was classical, but James didn't try to identify it. His eyes, his full attention, were on the staircase, waiting.

Then she was there, coming slowly down, her head high, huge eyes searching for him. She saw him, and her brilliant smile made him catch his breath.

She was exquisite, his Betsy. Her skin seemed to glow, and the golden lights in her auburn hair, piled high and back, caught and held the reflected light from the many lamps in the room, shining like a halo around her head as she reached the bottom of the stairs, her arm linked through Noah's. Her body was showcased by the shimmering silky gown, the high neck and long sleeves drawing attention to her lovely face, the rest of the gown slipping sensuously over her slender curves.

She came toward him on Noah's arm. The last of the notes of the violin faded and Noah stepped back, putting his arm around Annie. The minister's voice was deep and resonant.

"Dearly beloved, we are gathered here today—"

Off to one side, facing Betsy, Mary Elinora's fingers danced a graceful ballet as she turned the spoken words into sign.

James had eyes only for the woman at his side, and he made his vows directly to her, in sign and speech.

Then it was Betsy's turn.

"Elizabeth Mary Tompkins, do you take this man---"

Betsy turned toward him, a small, shy smile on her

lips. Her eyes held his, brimming with promise as her right hand made the yes sign, and with her voice she said clearly, "I do." Her closed hands then folded to her chest, telling him silently, passionately, of her love.

He slid the emerald ring, his great-grandmother's ring, on to Betsy's third finger. His mother had sent it, and with the ring had come loving messages from all his family, wishing him happiness, blessing this marriage, begging him and his bride to come for a visit. He'd talk it over with Betsy, and if she agreed, they'd go to Scotland in the spring.

"I now pronounce you husband and wife."

James heard the words, he saw the smiles and the tears on people's faces, he heard the applause begin and then swell around him and his wife. His wife. His beloved.

He bent his head and he kissed her, a silent promise, a prayer that their life together would be long and fruitful, and that the love and happiness they shared today would be with them both forevermore.

—THE END—

WANT TO KNOW WHAT ROSE GETS UP TO???

Find out in:
Rose's Mail Order Brides and Grooms:
Object—Matrimony
Western Prairie Brides, Book Three

Excerpt from
LANTERN IN THE WINDOW
Western Prairie Brides, Book One

Chapter One

February 22, 1886

"She's good and late. Prob'ly hit a blizzard."

The garrulous man also awaiting the arrival of the westbound train tugged his knitted cap closer around his ears and huddled into his woolen overcoat, eyeing Noah's heavy buffalo coat with envy. "That's some coat you got there, mister. You shoot the buffalo yer-self?"

Noah nodded, wishing the man would go pester someone else and leave him alone. He wasn't in any mood for small talk this afternoon.

"You a rancher hereabouts?"

Noah nodded again, a curt nod.

"Only just moved out here me'self," the man went on. "Don't know many folks yet, takes time. Name's Morris,

Henry Morris." He held out a mittened paw.

"Noah Ferguson." Noah shook the extended hand. Any other day, he'd have welcomed this stranger to the Canadian West, taken time to get to know him, but today he was too distracted.

"Nice meetin' ya, Ferguson. Waitin' on my wife Sadie and the kids, comin' out from the East," Morris confided, then waited expectantly.

When Noah didn't respond, Morris shifted from one foot to the other and then gave up. "Well, no sign of the train, and it looks like we're in fer a real blow, way that wind's pickin' up. Don't know about you, but I'm about freezin'. Why not come along inside the station house with the rest of us? No tellin' how late she'll be."

"Thanks. I'll be along presently." Relieved to be left alone, Noah thumped his mittens together and stamped his booted feet, pulling his scarf up and his weathered Western hat further down, painfully aware of the cold on his newly shaven cheeks and chin.

What the hell had possessed him to shave off his beard this morning? His rugged features might look better without all that wild black hair, but the beard might also have kept his chin from freezing, waiting for this damnable train.

And after all, what did he care how he might appear to her? It wasn't as if he had to court her; the marriage was over, the legal bond established between them. She had insisted on a proxy marriage before she left Toronto on the four-day train journey that was bringing her here to Medicine Hat. Against his better judgment—and the advice of the only lawyer in town—Noah had agreed.

He'd wanted it all over and done with. He'd signed the papers and sent the money for the fare, and now that she was almost here, his gut was churning. He wished to God the train would get here so they could be done with this awful first meeting, he and Annie Tompkins.

Annie Ferguson, he corrected himself. Annie Ferguson, his second wife. Tall, she'd described herself. Thirty-four, on the thin side, and plain, which suited him just fine. He'd been relieved to read her description of herself; after all, this was no love match, far from it.

Instead, it was a practical solution for them both. She was a soldier's wife, widowed in the Rebellion of 1885, a farm woman trapped in the city, working in some dingy factory to support herself and her young daughter while longing for the country life she'd known as a child.

And as for him, this marriage was a desperate measure.

He thought of his cranky, bed-ridden father, being cared for at this moment by a kindly neighbor, then deliberately forced his thoughts back to his new wife.

Redheaded, she'd said, which worried Noah some. Was it true, what they said about a redhead's temper? There'd been no sign of it in the eight letters she'd sent during the past months, and Lord only knew he had no experience of women's temper and no desire to learn.

Molly had been the sweetest of women. In their three years of marriage, Noah was hard put to recall times when she'd even come close to losing her temper.

Molly. Without warning, bitter rage at his loss welled up in him, rage so intense that his tall, well-muscled body trembled with the force of it, and he clenched his teeth and knotted his hands into fists inside the blue wool mittens his dead wife had knitted for him.

There were holes worn through one thumb and two fingers. Noah had clumsily mended them.

It had been two years now since Molly and his eighteen-month-old son, Jeremy, had died within hours of one another, victims of typhoid, and in recent months he'd begun to believe this smothering, impotent, choking fury was gone forever, that time had eased the agony of his loss. Instead, here it was back again, as powerful as ever, and now there was this gnawing guilt as well.

I never wanted any woman but you, Molly. Still don't, but I can't do it alone anymore, not since Dad had the stroke. If you'd lived, Molly, I wouldn't be in this damnable position, waiting to meet some stranger. I've had to invite her to share the house we built together, the bed we slept in. Damn it all, Molly, how could you do this to me?

He struggled for, and as always, recovered his self-control. He reminded himself with harsh honesty that his new wife would share as well the work of the ranch, the care of his father, the constant, ill-tempered demands of a once sweet natured man who'd become a tyrant since his stroke.

Noah swallowed hard and the last of the rage subsided, replaced with apprehension. He'd mentioned in his letters to Annie that his father wasn't well, but he'd never really explained exactly what taking care of Zachary involved. Hell, if he had done so, no woman in her right mind would have agreed to come, would she?

Like him, Annie and her young daughter would just have to make the best of this situation. He brushed one hand across his eyes, clearing away the snowflakes that blinded him, and squinted down the track.

Far off down the rails a single headlamp flickered in the driving snowstorm, and over the sound of the wind he could hear the eerie wail of the steam whistle and the sound of an approaching engine. The train was coming.

At last, the waiting was done.

With a screech of brakes and a cloud of steam, the engine groaned to a halt. Outside the passenger car, it was snowing heavily, but through the frosted window Annie could see a small knot of people on the platform, all staring expectantly up at the train.

An old man with a white beard was shoveling frantically to clear a path from the platform to the small wooden station.

"Med—i—c—ine Ha-a-a-t," the conductor called in

his sing-song fashion, making his way down the crowded aisle to open the door.

After four endless days riding across empty wilderness, at last they'd arrived. Heart thumping so hard she was certain it would fly out of her chest, Annie tried to adjust the flamboyant hat Elinora had given her as a parting gift, but it wouldn't stay put.

Bets reached out and straightened it, and Annie gave her a grateful smile and a wink, trying to pretend a bravado she was far from feeling. With trembling hands she gathered their bundles together, wrapped Bets's wool shawl tighter around her, and followed the other departing passengers to the door.

Tilting her chin high, Annie lifted her skirts and stepped down into snow on legs that had turned to jelly.

Lordie, it was freezing. She paused and caught her breath as the cold air seared her lungs. Once the first shock was over, however, the icy air felt clean and invigorating after the stuffy train compartment, but it started Bets to coughing again.

Annie twisted her sister's scarf up and over her chin and mouth, and then, feeling sick with nerves, she squinted into the snow and tried to pick out which of the men waiting a short distance away might be Noah Ferguson.

Thirty-six years old, he'd written. Tall, dark-haired.

Her eyes skittered past a short, round figure with a cable knit hat pulled down to his eyelids, lingered on a thin, red-faced man with a handlebar moustache and a brimmed cap, and then settled on the giant standing like a statue a little distance from the others, brimmed hat hiding his face, hands thrust deep into the pockets of a huge furry coat. Annie looked, and looked again.

Some sixth sense told her that this was her husband.

His gaze touched her face and flicked past her, to the passenger car where a very fat woman with several children was now being helped down the step. "Sadie," bellowed the man in the knitted hat, racing over and throwing his arms around her.

There were no other passengers getting off. The conductor was closing the door.

The man in the heavy coat looked at Annie again, puzzlement in his frown, and Annie swallowed hard and said a silent, fervent prayer as he moved towards her.

Lordie, he was big. She was tall for a woman, but he towered over her. There was a ruggedness and raw strength about him unfamiliar to Annie, accustomed as she was to city men.

She drew herself up and squared her shoulders, praying that she didn't look as terrified as she felt. She attempted a smile and knew it was a dismal failure.

"How do you do?" Her voice was barely audible.

His face was all angles and planes, a stern, strong, handsome face, clean shaven and unsmiling.

"I'm looking for Miss Annie Tompkins. Rather, Mrs.

Annie Ferguson," he corrected. His voice was a deep baritone.

"That's me," she managed to say. She tried again to smile, but her lips felt paralyzed. "I'm Annie, and this is my—this is Bets."

Bets, her wide, feverish blue gaze intent on Noah's face, made a small curtsy and then edged fearfully behind her sister, doing her best to stifle her coughing and not succeeding.

Annie cleared her throat, desperately trying to remember the dignified little speech she'd been preparing every anxious moment since she'd left Toronto. Not one word came to her.

"Hello, Noah Ferguson," she finally managed to stammer. "Pleased to meet you, I'm sure," she choked out, painfully aware that she sounded both weak-minded and simpering.

He didn't respond. Instead, his coal-dark eyes slowly took in her hat, her face, then her figure. He looked her up and down. Annie refused to flinch under his gaze. She clenched her teeth as he stepped around her to stare at Bets before he once again turned his attention to Annie.

"You're considerably younger than you led me to believe, madam. How old are you, exactly?" He was scowling down at her, and a shiver ran down her spine that had nothing to do with the snow swirling around them.

Here it was then, the first consequence of all her lying.

There was nothing to be done except confront it head on.

"I'm twenty-two." Annie tilted her chin as high as she could and met his coal-dark eyes, but after a long moment under his steady gaze, her bravado crumbled.

"Well, almost twenty-two. I'll be twenty-one this June." At the thunderous look on his face, she hurriedly added, "I know you wanted someone older, Mr. Ferguson. I was afraid if I told the truth, you wouldn't have me. Us. But I assure you, I feel a lot older inside than my years. If that's any help."

He actually snorted in disgust. He looked from her to Bets and back again. "Twenty years old. And with a fourteen-year-old daughter? That's quite an accomplishment, madam." His voice dripped with sarcasm.

If it weren't so cold, Annie would have sworn this was hell.

"She's—Bets is my little sister, not my daughter," she confessed miserably. "I—I've never been married. I thought you might not—I thought—"

He stared at her until she gulped and was silent. "You thought I was fair game, and you told me only what you figured I wanted to hear. I take it most of what you've told me about yourself is nothing but a pack of lies. Is that so, madam?"

His voice was quiet, but lethal.

Annie desperately wanted to contradict him, but couldn't. The fact was, a great deal of what she'd told him was a pack of lies. There was no denying it.

"Some," she admitted miserably. "The part about growing up on a farm wasn't exactly honest. But the part about me and Bets being hard workers, that's the god-honest truth," she burst out. "We worked from dawn to dusk in Lazenby's cotton mill, anybody could tell you we were among the best. Just give us a chance, and we'll prove it to you, Mr. Ferguson, I promise we will."

"If I'd wanted farmhands, I'd have hired men." He looked as though he was about to explode, and Annie steeled herself.

Bets had been choking back her coughing, but now it took hold of her with a vengeance and she doubled over, her face purple.

Annie drew the smaller girl close against her side and felt Bets's whole body trembling. The wind had picked up and the snow was swirling around them.

Annie had been too distraught to even feel the cold, but now it suddenly thrust icy fingers past the inadequate barrier of her clothing, and she was miserably aware that the soles on her boots were worn through in places, letting the snow in.

"My sister's sick, Mr. Ferguson. She caught the grippe on the train, and we're both freezing cold. Please, couldn't we talk this over at some later time?"

Annie knew the moment had come when he could—probably would—turn his back on them and simply walk away. She knew he'd be well within his rights to do that very thing, leaving them to fend for themselves in a snowstorm in the middle of the wild Canadian west.

Desperation gripped her. If he left them, what in God's name would she do? She had little money left; she knew no one in this barren, savage place. All she'd ever done was work in the cotton mill, and she was pretty certain there were no mills within a thousand miles of here.

She was terrified. She trembled with fear, and her stomach churned. She clutched Bets's arm so tightly that the girl cried out.

Ferguson's eyes held hers for what seemed an eternity, and with her last vestige of courage, Annie stared straight back, willing him—begging him, entreating him—to give her a chance.

Books in the Doctor 911 Series:

DRASTIC MEASURES
PICKING CLOVER
NURSING THE DOCTOR
PATIENT CARE
BABY DOCTOR
ARE YOU MY DADDY?
FULL RECOVERY
DOUBLE JEOPARDY

Other books by Bobby Hutchinson:

HIS GUARDIAN ANGEL
LANTERN IN THE WINDOW
FOLLOW A WILD HEART
A LEGAL AFFAIR
ISLAND SUNRISE
SPECIAL EDUCATION
HOW NOT TO RUN A B&B
ALMOST AN ANGEL
GRADY'S KIDS
LOVE OF A RODEO MAN
KNIGHTS OF THE NORTH
NOW AND THEN

About the Author

Bobby Hutchinson was born in Sparwood, a small town in interior British Columbia. Her father was an underground coalminer, her mother, a housewife, and both were storytellers. Learning to read was the most significant event in her early life.

Bobby married young and had three sons; the middle child was deaf, and he taught her patience. After twelve years, she divorced and worked at various odd jobs, directing traffic around construction sites; day caring challenged children; and selling fabric, by the pound, at a remnant store.

Following this, she mortgaged her house and bought the

remnant store. Accompanied by her sewing machine, she began to sew one dress a day. The dresses sold, the fabric didn't, so she hired four seamstresses and turned the old remnant store into a boutique.

After twelve successful years, Bobby sold the business and decided to run a marathon. Training was a huge bore, so she made up a story about Pheiddipedes, the first marathoner, as she ran. She copied it down and sent it to Chatelaine Magazine's short story contest, won first prize, and became a writer.

Bobby remarried and divorced again, writing all the while. Today, she has dozens of published books on Amazon, Smashwords, Kobo and I Tunes and currently is working on three or four more. She has six enchanting grandchildren and lives alone.

Bobby walks a lot, does yoga, meditates, reads endlessly, takes advice from her grandchildren, and likes this quote by Dolly Parton: "Decide who you are, and then do it on purpose."

Visit Bobby's Website: http://www.bobbyhutchinson.ca/
Read Bobby's Blog: http://bobbyhutchinson.ca/blogs/
Join Bobby on Facebook:
    http://www.facebook.com/BobbyHutchinsonBooks
Follow Bobby on Twitter: @bluecollarbobby

Made in United States
Orlando, FL
01 November 2021

10151421R00111